W🐾LF
SUMMER

W✧LF SUMMER

a novel

ROB KEOUGH

GREAT PLAINS
TEEN FICTION

Great Plains Teen Fiction
(an imprint of Great Plains Publications)
420–70 Arthur Street
Winnipeg, MB R3B 1G7
www.greatplains.mb.ca

Great Plains Publications gratefully acknowledges the financial support provided for its publishing program by the Government of Canada through the Book Publishing Industry Development Program (BPIDP); the Canada Council for the Arts; as well as the Manitoba Department of Culture, Heritage and Tourism; and the Manitoba Arts Council.

Design & Typography by Relish Design Studios Ltd.

Printed in Canada by Friesens Printing

LIBRARY AND ARCHIVES CANADA CATALOGUING IN PUBLICATION

Keough, Rob
        Wolf summer / Rob Keough.
ISBN 978-1-894283-87-8
I. Title.
PS8621.E68W65 2009   jC813'.6   C2008-907064-X

Mixed Sources
Cert no. SW-COC-001271
© 1996 FSC

FSC

ENVIRONMENTAL BENEFITS STATEMENT

Great Plains Publications saved the following resources by printing the pages of this book on chlorine free paper made with 100% post-consumer waste.

TREES	WATER	ENERGY	SOLID WASTE	GREENHOUSE GASES
10	3,640	7	467	877
FULLY GROWN	GALLONS	MILLION BTUs	POUNDS	POUNDS

Calculations based on research by Environmental Defense and the Paper Task Force. Manufactured at Friesens Corporation

*To Mom & Dad who loaded up a Buick LeSabre
station wagon with four kids and two dogs every
weekend to drive out to the lake.*

*And to Ella Jayne, whose Mom & Dad
are headed in the same direction.*

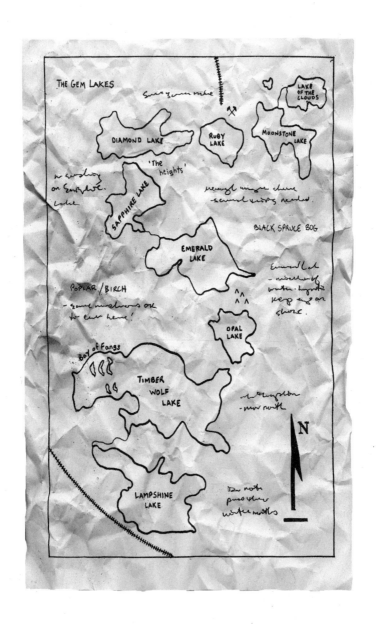

RUSTY'S MAP

Jake's
Map

Part One

A NEARLY FROZEN CROW ruffled his shiny black feathers to shake off a skim of icy snow. He'd left the sheltered confines of his nest deep in the forest to investigate movement on this night when there should only have been stillness. The observant bird was not surprised to see that the source of motion was Jake Lucknow, who he'd been keeping a keen eye on since last summer. It was now the following April, and the old bird saw that young Mr. Lucknow had made a choice that he would have strongly advised against.

An early spring blizzard had whipped up from the prairies in the west, and was swirling and whirling around the boy like a frigid hurricane. He *should* have stayed in his grandfather's cabin, which was warm, and cozy—and more to the point, safe—nestled on the north shore of the frozen Lake of the Clouds. But, he did not.

Instead, Jake had made it halfway across the lake, and was tramping through thigh-high snow, fighting a bitter wind that had a physical force to it. His eyebrows were long stretches of frost and ice, and he was blocking the blinding snow with his arm, making it that much more awkward to walk. Jake was exhausted. Despite the cold, he felt sweat forming on his neck and the back of his knees. When he stopped, even for a moment, the dampness began to freeze. His mule-like stubbornness was the only thing that kept him from turning around to find the soft glowing light from the cabin's windows. With the blizzard, he would be unlikely to make out the light anyway.

Muscles in Jake's legs began to ache and quiver. He'd realized early on that he was in trouble, and that going out in this kind of weather had been crazy. But it wasn't like he'd had a choice.

The winter berries had been buried by three consecutive snowstorms and deep snow had made it impossible to get around without snowshoes to hunt grouse or rabbit. Jake had a pair, but had yet to master the art of actually *walking* in them, and so had found himself without food very quickly. His grandfather was tending his traplines, and was supposed to be gone for three or four days. This night marked the tenth day since Rusty Lucknow had left and Jake could not stand it for one second longer. Although he was pretty certain that his grandfather's movement had been slowed by the unrelenting storms, he couldn't shake a very bad feeling.

By the time this storm had begun several hours ago, Jake had already worked himself into a frazzled mess. His imagination had churned out a thousand different hazards that his grandfather could have succumbed to, each one worse than the next. As the wind picked up and the snow started blowing, Jake had bundled into all the heavy clothing he could manage, screwed on some courage and pushed his way out onto the lake in search of the missing man.

The snow was not nearly as deep in the middle of the lake because the wind was sweeping it into heavy drifts along the shore and Jake could feel that the ice was not nearly as solid as he had previously assumed. In fact, somewhere in the last several yards, it had become slushy and he noticed puddles of grey snow.

The ice did not even crack when he suddenly plummeted down into the terrible cold of the lake. Instead it made the sound that wet cardboard would if you were to press your hand through it. Jake did what his grandfather had taught him to do in such situations and stuck his arms out straight sideways to catch some solid ice. Rusty's most sound advice, *Keep off the ice in the spring; it's unpredictable,* blared from the back of his head.

Unfortunately Jake had wandered over a patch of thin and brittle ice, forced that way by the insulating effects of two feet of snow. His arms broke through the thin crust as well, and Jake was well on his way to making this fourteenth year his last.

His layers of clothing instantly tripled in weight and pulled his head under the surface. It was a shocking cold that pulsed straight through to his internal organs. His heart jumped in fear. His body numbed instantaneously and he swallowed two healthy mouthfuls of liquid ice that clamped shut his throat.

Jake thrashed wildly in the frigid black water knowing full well that even if he did manage to pull himself out that there was no way he could drag himself home. He had survived the entire winter and then killed himself in twenty minutes of sheer stupidity. He realized that his arms had stopped moving and he was sinking. The water was so, so cold.

The violent pull on the back of Jake's hooded jacket came the moment before his wide-open eyes slipped beneath the black surface.

"What in *blue blazes* are you doing out here?" Rusty Lucknow roared through the howling wind. The words were ripped out of his mouth and vanished quickly in the storm, so Jake only comprehended every other word. The words he *did* hear pierced deeper than the ice pellets that were whipping his red skin.

Icicles hung from the old man's frosted beard in impossibly long lengths. His blue eyes were harder than steel. He was shaking with anger.

Rusty may have been ninety years old but he was still as strong as a plow ox. He held Jake up three feet above the ice with his only hand—his right one lost to a wildcat years before—still by the scruff of his neck, dangling in the air like a soundless wind chime. Ice crusted on Jake's pants and jacket immediately. He could *feel* his lips turning blue.

Behind Rusty, a dark mound lay on the snow that Jake could not identify until the old man stooped to retrieve it. Hares—giant ones, a common effect of the magnetic field that extended throughout the Gem Lakes Range.

The last thought that passed through Jake's mind before he closed his eyes was of hot rabbit stew.

Rusty Lucknow dragged his well intentioned but ill-prepared grandson back to the cabin on the old wooden sled he had been pulling by a harness on his back. To make room he reluctantly untied a few hundred pounds of partially frozen meat and left it on the ice. He would retrieve it later if the wolves didn't find it first.

The old man covered the distance in a quarter of the time that his grandson took in getting across the lake by avoiding the grainy, powdery snow and finding a path of crusty, crunchy "rotten" snow that had partially melted and then refrozen. It made for good traction.

He would have made even better time if he hadn't stopped two or three times to smack Jake upside the head to keep him from sleeping.

By the time Rusty made it to the bottom of the snow-drifted stairs he had to carry his grandson into the cabin because Jake couldn't feel his own legs. He kicked the door open and gently placed Jake on the floor in front of the fireplace.

Jake tried to curl into the fetal position but found it impossible with his clothes frozen stiff. If he had ever been more uncomfortable he could not remember it. Worse, his grandfather was clearly not happy, cussing like a bandit and making no apologies for it either—something about being gone too long, something else about a lack of common sense, and some *very* strong mumbling about leaving hard-earned meat in the middle of the lake.

Rusty plucked a wooden match from the tin on the shelf above the table, scraped it across the gritty sandpaper he had stuck with tree sap to the tin bottom, and lit the wick to the kerosene lantern that hung from above.

The meagre heat coming from the fire in the stove did little to penetrate Jake's frozen skin. His fingers couldn't work the buttons and ties of his jacket, and as Rusty moved back and forth stoking the fire and filling four metal pails with snow and setting them on the woodstove he aimed random unpleasantries in Jake's direction. "Where did you think you were goin'? Harebrained idea is what it was! There's enough trouble in these parts that you don't have to go *lookin'* for it ya know!"

He took the wool blanket from the bed and hung it on the nail on the wall behind the fire. He pulled a large tin basin out and poured the melted snow in.

By that time Jake had managed to pull off his drenched clothes and they sat in a steaming lump on the floor. He was shivering uncontrollably and his skin looked as pale and clammy as a fish belly.

"You're not out of trouble yet boy. Hypothermia is just around the corner. Get in the basin."

Jake stepped in and couldn't even feel the water. He submerged his hands hoping to get feeling back in them first. "No, no—warm the core first. All that cold blood in your hands and feet will go straight to your heart and kill you faster than a silver bullet."

So Jake sat in the tub of water with his arms and legs dangling ridiculously over the edge. He stared up at the ceiling and waited for the feeling to come back to his body. His brain was beginning to function again. He looked around the cabin and took in the surroundings he now shared with his somewhat newly discovered grandfather.

After Jake's decision to stay in the Gem Lakes, the issue of accommodations turned out to be moot until the temperature had started to fall. Jake stayed in the cabin and Rusty usually fell asleep outside either on the porch or in a lean-to somewhere in the forest while he checked traplines. When the snow started to fall they had become somewhat reluctant roommates—only inasmuch that Jake felt he was completely invading his grandfather's space.

The inside of the cabin had indeed become a bit of a squeeze since Jake had moved in. A small metal bed frame now occupied the wall beside the door that only left six inches of space between the foot of the bed and the woodstove. They had spent a day dragging the frame from the Succa Sunna Mine and spent another day scraping the rust off of it. For the mattress they had salvaged whatever material wasn't soaked in mould and pieced it together to make a cover and had aired it out for seven full days to get the must and dust out of it. They had filled it with pine boughs and although Jake had had his doubts about its comfort potential it turned out to be easily the most comfy bed he had ever had the pleasure of sleeping in. He wanted to crawl into it right now and not come out until summer.

Jake had also absconded with a fairly good-sized wooden trunk from the mine that now held his ragged collection of clothes. Those clothes included the bundle from the Lucknow cabin closet that his grandfather had mysteriously reappeared with after a solo canoe trip in the late fall last year. To make more floor space everything from basins, bowls and cups to axes and hatchets and boots were now fastened to the walls or stowed under beds; yet the cabin never felt cluttered, only comfortable. Like a home.

Jake looked down to see his flesh had flared pink, which he hoped was a good sign. He looked over at the fireplace, which was now choked full of logs, the flames lapping against the metal and hissing blessed heat.

His grandfather sat in the wooden chair. Water droplets clung to his beard and dripped on his lap. He did not look angry anymore. It was something else. Not disappointment, but relief. It brought a lump to Jake's throat to see it.

On the last day of April, winter's resilient grasp finally began to let go although it was not until late May that the snow and ice in the deep bush finally melted away. Jake was glad to see it go. The month of February had been so brutally cold that Jake had only left the cabin to use the biffy. Yellow snow had encircled the cabin.

Crooked strings of snow geese filled the sky daily, passing through on their way home from Texas or California or whatever other sunny retreat they wintered at. Jake often wished one of them would drop dead of a heart attack and fall into his lap. He craved any meat other than rabbit, which had officially come off the menu anyway when the snow melted. When their white coats moulted back to brown they became impossible to see and thusly impossible to catch. At least in the winter their distinctive tracks gave them away.

Although the cabin had a primitive root cellar that held a decent supply of potatoes, radishes and wild onions, a man in his most basic form was a carnivore and Jake got moody if it became too long a time between meats. The moose that Rusty had killed in the early autumn did not dry properly and half the meat was lost before winter started. The remaining roast was gone by mid-January much to the astonishment of Rusty who couldn't believe how much his scrawny grandson could eat in one sitting. "You are a pig" was muttered good-naturedly over many a late night dinner.

The new diet had been an enormous adjustment on Jake's stomach, which had not initially taken well to the unprocessed, unseasoned world of wild food. He would sometimes go days without a meal although it was not for lack of options. Twice his grandfather had offered him something that looked like shiny candy that turned out to be fish eyeballs. "I'll tell you what," he had told him, "if it comes down to me sucking the liquid out of eyeballs or dying, I'll see you on the other side."

"You say that now," Rusty had retorted.

When Jake was lucky enough to be dining on fresh fish or juicy grouse or even a gamey tasting goose, he took great care to enjoy every morsel.

When he was forced to eat something else like plant roots or fox livers he liked to be doing something else while he snacked to distract himself of the fact he was eating plant roots or fox livers.

They did have two food caches, one of which was the rudimentary cellar that was just a hole dug deeply under the front porch. It certainly kept things cool but there was no room for anything substantial and it was a chore to keep the food covered from bugs and mice.

The second was a more elaborate structure that looked like a tree house, mainly because that's where it was perched. You could access the cache through the floor after climbing up the trunk that had old two by fours nailed into it. It was perfect for their needs except for one thing: it was currently empty.

While the cabin itself was remarkably well built Jake had learned through the spring that it was by no means an architectural marvel. There was obviously no sealant around the windows and drafts could be felt in several spots if he ran his hand over the walls. The roof leaked in the area where the stovepipe went through the roof and when it rained the drops would boil on the top of the steel.

Outside the cabin walls, wildflowers were pushing their way through the stubborn crusts of snow and green buds were already sprouting on every barren tree.

Jake compared the scene to back in the city where a winter's worth of sand and salt would be heaped in ragged piles by the curbs, the sidewalks were a minefield of thawed out dog droppings and half-frozen candy wrappers, and the city's two landfills would be thawing into steaming piles of garbage. The warmer it became the more it would smell and the more sea gulls and crows would feast on a season's worth of rot.

In the forest, the creeks and hollows that had been carved out by ancient glaciers swelled up with melt water, creating a window of chance for unprecedented travel opportunities. In springtime one could get around the Gem Lake Range as easily as a small city. The runoff turned the forest into a network of fast paced water canals.

The problem was, if you were not yet skilled enough in the art of paddling, as Jake was not, then the rushing water had a way of carrying the canoe wherever it pleased: sideways, backward or dead-ahead.

There was a brief interruption in the transportation process as the ice became too brittle to walk on. Jake and his grandfather woke up one morning to find that the ice had pulled away from the shoreline. The snow had all crystallized on the surface and shimmered like a blanket of jewels. When the wind picked up around noon Rusty declared that the water would be wide open by nightfall. He was right. The warm wind carved pockets in the ice, which caused large chunks to break off at a time. Once, Jake threw a rock out onto a floating chunk and the rock punched a hole right through it.

As the snow slowly melted it also revealed the activity of the animals during the winter season. Still frozen and preserved carcasses dotted the landscape, some of which had perished by starvation, others because they were too late to take shelter from the cold, and others that were half-eaten from predation.

One carcass in particular held the crow's interest and he saw that his concerns about the mighty *joaquin* coming back from the dead turned out to be unfounded.

The mythical cat that ended up being more muscle than myth had terrorized Jake and his sister, Claire, last summer. For decades before it had existed as a seldom seen silent killer—until the night it tore through the walls of their tent, and the Lucknow boy had hit the mark with the thin blade of his filleting knife.

After Jake's unlikely if not fortuitous defeat of the monster, the joaquin corpse was unceremoniously dumped into the bush. If it had been any other animal the bugs and the scavengers would have reduced it to a pile of bones within days. What had developed, however, could turn out to be a very pressing problem.

The joaquin was left undisturbed by insect and animal alike right up until the first snowfall many months later. In turn it was left to mummify in the hot sun, and the stench of death that came off the great beast was not really death at all but something far worse.

A dark blue sludge oozed out of its nostrils and from the knife wound that brought it down. This was the source of that smell that was masking death's powerful scent.

After lying in state under the snow for six months the smell had dissipated somewhat and now the big cat that had slaughtered so many people for so many years gave off a tangy odour similar to a rotting fruitcake.

It did not take long for a pack of wolves to find the now bloated corpse. Six hundred pounds of decaying meat had a way of attracting attention in these parts. Black flies were circling the beast, and if the body were rolled over, it was more than likely that the maggots had joined the party as well.

These wolves looked to be a group from the Moonstone pack, most with the same golden hue of the ones that guided the Lucknow brood through the night last year. Their leader was black as coal. His dark hair stood on end as he sized up the situation.

The wolf pack had experienced a very long winter and the snow had been so deep all season that it had come up to their chests, making it virtually impossible for them to hunt together. They had moved in single-file almost all winter and had lost more body weight than they could afford. In fact one of the younger members of the pack had not made it through and had dropped dead of hunger as they were crossing a large windswept lake. They had left him, and were too exhausted to even look back.

Now the remaining pack of six circled the lifeless cat wearily as if it were only playing dead. They had reason to be nervous, as the joaquin had taken down four from their group over the years. The scent of the great animal still lingered but it had definitely changed. It seemed stale. Soon though their gnawing hunger was enough to overcome their fear and they tore into their meal with ravenous abandon.

The wolves devoured their only predator, along with the vile blue tar that had bubbled through the joaquin's bloodstream, with reckless abandon.

The tar was evil, and would poison these fine animals just as it had the joaquin, their present meal.

Jake woke up in a groggy state, his grandfather's hand on his shoulder, shaking him awake. Through the slits in his eyes he could see the first beams of the morning sun filtering through the window. "What is it?" he managed to grunt.

"Get up and come with me, but be quiet. Hurry up now!"

Jake reluctantly left the warm comfort of his bed, and swung his legs over the edge. He cringed as his bare feet hit the cool floor. He was already wearing a white long-sleeved shirt. He found a pair of dirty wool socks, and tugged on the ancient oil-stained snowmobile pants that he had inherited from his grandfather's collection of bush clothes. He retrieved two leather boots from under the bed, and slowly pulled them on. He was as ready as he was going to be at that hour of the morning.

The cool morning air smacked him in the face. He could see the mist of his breath and the ground crunched underneath his feet while he walked. Plunging his hands deep into his pockets, he somewhat grumpily followed Rusty Lucknow behind the cabin and through the forest. For some reason, this morning, Rusty had decided to stray off the beaten path. He was careful to hold back any branches that threatened to whip Jake in his face.

They came to a watering hole that Jake had only been to once before. The white moon still hung low in the crisp sky like it had forgotten it was supposed to go down. It shone like a crystal ball. Frozen swords of reeds rimmed the entire lake and a dusting of frost tipped each and every one of them like powdered sugar. A very thin crust of ice still filmed the shallow water but Jake held his breath as he saw what it was that his grandfather was showing him.

The entire lake was filled with Canadian Geese — *thousands* of them. Some of them were huge but most were typical sized, not being in the Gem Lake Range long enough to be affected by any magnetic fields. The birds were honking quietly and yapping at each other. When the sun came over the trees the geese would take off en masse.

After ten minutes of marvelling at the sight in front of them Rusty formed a mischievous grin on his face. He pried a pebble from the cold mud and rolled it around his fingers. It was no bigger than a marble. He tossed it gently in the air and it plunked into the water between two of the geese. The birds roared from the lake with a terrible din — first the ones closest to them, then the middle, and then the ones from the far end of the lake like a rising tidal wave. Jake had to cover his ears to muffle the noise, but could not look away if he wanted to. He had not seen a sight like this in his entire life. His breath caught in his throat.

His grandfather was clearly not as enamoured with the
moment as he had rambled out into the shallow mud,
breaking through thin ice and striking his good arm out like
a harpoon as the birds had lifted. It was one of many moments where Jake thought his grandpa was losing his mind.
"Pretty cool show eh? This whole lake is filled with wild
rice. It's their favourite."
Jake just nodded his head. He saw that his grandfather
had a very large goose by the neck. It was dead. He should
have known that Rusty would not have made a mere sight-
seeing trip and he certainly wouldn't wait around for his
potential dinner to have a heart attack.
"Did you pick the biggest one or what?"
"Nope, just the slowest."

The water many miles south, in the cottage community of
Lampshine Lake, rippled slightly in a warm mid-day breeze;
one of those spring fresh winds that seemed to breathe life
back into everything that had wilted during the winter dol-
drums, and provided a tantalizing preview of the balmy
summer weather ahead.
It was a time of revival in the lake community as well.
After the road committee had inspected the private road for
winter damage and softness, they had declared it open for
the first weekend in May: opening weekend.
All around the lake cottagers were taking down their
wooden shutters, checking out how many mice had wintered in their respective cabins and hauling the heavy propane tanks back and forth across the lake, replacing the
empties with fresh, full ones.

There were outboard motors to tune up and boats to launch. There was deadfall to cut and stack. A few people had not pulled their docks out of the water the previous fall, instead gambling that the ice would not damage them as it pulled away from the shore. Those people were now scouring the shoreline for pieces of their ravaged decks and twisted frames.

Bob Lucknow stretched out his pale sun-starved legs on his faded lounge chair and watched the black fly that was buzzing around his head settle on his kneecap like a miniature helicopter. He rolled up a magazine into a tight cylinder and held it above his head. The fly tickled his skin as it fretted and hopped about, totally unaffected by the mild breeze coming in off the lake.

With a quick snap of his wrist Bob brought the glossy weapon down hard and yelped in pain as he hit his mark. Despite the self-sacrifice the fly would no longer be an annoyance.

Across from him, sunning herself in the noon-hour sun was Susan, wearing a floppy baby-blue hat and matching sunglasses. He couldn't tell if she was sleeping or not but he would have bet that she was. It had been a very long year for his wife. Bob had tried in vain to tell her about his father, explain about the magnetic field that lay behind their summer home and that Jake was in fact alive and well and safe in the forest behind them. It had not gotten through a mother's protective heart. *How do you know he's safe? How could you possibly know?* At first, Susan had let fly a string of colourful language—mostly tinted a decided shade of blue—every time he had brought up the subject of Gordon Lucknow.

Rob Keough

She had demanded the RCMP Search and Rescue team go in and try to find him and they had tried valiantly for five weeks before calling off the search due to the extreme danger involved.

As part of her debriefing last year she knew that the six lakes—Opal, Emerald, Sapphire, Diamond, Ruby and Moonstone—sat in the south end of a magnetic field that was the root cause of a bevy of abnormalities that included enlarged and aggressive animals, albino pigments, boiling lakes. It was also the only reason that Susan hadn't buried her son last summer.

The Gem Lakes, and more specifically the magnetically mutated animals that lived there, had claimed more human lives than the Bermuda Triangle but was nowhere near as notorious. The Canadian government worked very hard to make sure of that. It wasn't as if the magnetic range was buried under Toronto or Montreal. The area was so remote that the only people they had to worry about were the cottagers on Lampshine Lake.

The government could not possibly patrol the area as it was much too large and they found they didn't have to, as local legend scared most people off. No trapping permits or hunting was allowed in the range.

There had apparently been consideration of levelling the cabins on Lampshine and evicting the cottagers, but the uproar would no doubt trigger national attention. It was better to let sleeping dogs lie.

The entire five weeks went by agonizingly slow as each day something else went wrong with the search. First the radios wouldn't work: short wave, long wave, cellular phone,

27

they were all rendered useless over the heavy magnet that was buried deep beneath the lakes. With no communication the whole operation was doomed from the start.

Susan already knew the area was a no-fly zone as airplane instruments died shortly after entering the airspace north of Opal Lake. The ground search was nearly impossible through the vast stretch of land and on four separate occasions men were hauled back to the base camp at the parking lot in stretchers. Not one person disclosed what had caused any injuries, although Susan had caught sight of one man returning with an ear ripped off his head.

Through it all, she knew that Major Duncan Shocklot was holed up in his underground bunker somewhere, pulling the strings of the entire search. No doubt he was letting her think that they were putting out a full effort when they were just gathering more information for his sealed classified files. During a debriefing last summer, the major and his military cronies had let it be known that if she brought undo attention to the lakes that they would make very sure that she was admitted to some sort of facility for "therapy." They also kindly reminded her that she had another child to raise, and she might be more interested in focusing on that.

She refused to believe the searchmaster until finally Claire herself had sat down with her—alone—and gave an eyewitness account of what she had seen in the Gem Lakes.

It was clear that Claire had only made it out alive because of Rusty's personal escort. He had taken her all the way to the Opal Portage and made sure she made it to the top of the hill that led down to Timber Wolf. For that Susan was grateful to Rusty. The fact he did not bring Jake back as well burned that gratitude to ashes. She understood that Jake was healthier staying behind, but it didn't change the way she felt. She missed her son. A big part of her would rather have had him home.

Claire was off visiting Susan's parents in Nova Scotia this spring and would not be back until June. That was by design. Time would heal all wounds and indeed, Lampshine would once again become a source of healing and comfort for Claire. Eventually. But right now, opening weekend, it was much too soon. She had not wanted to come back to the lake this early and face bad news that maybe Jake had not made it through the winter. She didn't know for sure if Rusty would contact her dad if the news was bad but she thought he would.

The truth was, Bob had felt the same way. Prairie winters were merciless. The two-hour car ride from the city had felt more like ten. Bob and Susan had ricocheted between excruciating silence and mindless conversation to keep their thoughts off what was waiting behind the road gate. Susan had nearly convinced Bob to take the train down in the winter and try to take a snowmobile into the lakes, but Bob had tried that before years ago when trying to visit his father.

The snowmobile had died. Bob had to walk back all the way from the bear caves—thankfully, the bears were hibernating. He nearly got frostbite and he never saw that snowmobile again. He had nothing to go back and tow it with; he assumed that during the next spring thaw it had sunk to the bottom of the lake it had stalled on.

As the water gently lapped up against the dock that he'd recently reinstalled in the shallow but cold water, Bob carefully flattened out his magazine and let out a grunt of distress. The black fly had the last laugh as its guts and gore had smeared all over the perfectly airbrushed face of a female tennis player that could have doubled as a runway model. Susan, apparently not asleep after all, choked on a chuckle.

The woodpile behind the cabin on the Lake of the Clouds, at the top of the chain of Gem Lakes, had been critically depleted over the long winter. The cabin's only insulation was the dried mud mixture that had been used as chinking between the logs. The windows bled heat especially when the north wind kicked up and Jake had worn a weary trail between the pile and the cabin door all winter. The long-burning rockwood that Jake had hoped would help them sail through the winter left thick and gritty deposits in the chimney that once caused the stovepipe to glow red for three hours and threatened to burn the entire cabin down. After that incident the woodstove had consumed the woodpile in ferocious fashion and now Jake was looking at just a few loose sticks and the last layer of logs that had been frozen into the ground. It was a pathetic sight and a situation that warranted top priority.

With no chainsaw available he set about looking for dead fall first, hoping to find some good trees that had fallen over the windy winter. He found lots of old wood that was too rotten and mushy to be useful but also managed to discover a few thin Jack pines within short dragging distance. Later he would hunt for some thicker trees and work on chopping them down himself. Each full tree he felled required cleaning off the branches—which he kept and dried out for kindling—and then cutting into stove size pieces with an old band saw. It was hard but necessary work.

An empty jar sat in the grass that Jake would fill with homemade toothpicks from the slivers of cordwood that would litter the ground after the day's cutting. They would be washed, boiled and then dried in the sun after being cut down to the suitable lengths. Without toothbrushes, they were great for getting a gristly piece of wild game from one's molar.

Rusty appeared from the forest behind him and waved him over. "Grab a bucket. It's our lucky day!"

Jake grabbed a dented metal pail with no handle and followed Rusty into the woods. He had learned that what constituted a "lucky day" to his grandfather did not necessary match his own definition.

Wild mushrooms flowed down the side of a creek bed into the gravelly bottom where some truly gigantic ones were thriving in the cold water.

Rusty spread his arms wide. "This," he declared, "is a delicacy. I can make a splendid sauce for our goose." He walked barefoot into the shallow water and started picking the larger ones, carefully inspecting each one as if he was picking fruit at a supermarket.

Jake moved through the knee-deep grass and started picking through the ones on dry ground. He was always happy to add new flavours to the menu.

"I don't want to see you pick'n mushrooms on your own boy. Most of 'em will kill you in a most unpleasant way."

Between the two of them they picked an overflowing bucket of the fungus in no time. Rusty went down to the lake to wash their newfound treasures and Jake went back to his wooding. This was a commonplace event for the two lately. Jake and Rusty would go about their own business for the most part, and when Rusty felt there was something valuable to teach his young grandson he would make a point of it. The student, for his part, was a fast and eager learner.

As he dropped a smallish Jack pine onto his homemade sawhorse Jake brushed his sticky forehead with his arm and noticed that it was streaked with mud. The mud seemed to be moving. Jake realized quickly that it was not mud at all.

Streams of wood ticks—hundreds and hundreds of them—were crawling all over him. A wave of nausea passed over him and his head felt like it was sinking into his shoulders. He frantically wiped them off but even still some had already burrowed their heads into his skin. He saw a batch marching up his arm towards his shoulder and whipped his shirt off. There were more wood ticks on his chest, in his belly button and more making a beeline to his face. He ripped his pants off to find his legs beneath the knee covered with ticks. He bolted towards the lake like he was on fire.

Rusty was kneeling by the water when his half-naked grandson tore by him in a blur, stepped directly in the now empty bucket and hurled-tripped himself into the water. The lake was still icy cold from the spring thaw and Jake gasped for warm air as he burst to the surface.

"It's tick season. You should wear long pants," Rusty noted.

"Now you tell me!" he sputtered.

"There's a leech on your forehead," the old man observed helpfully. Jake screamed and tore out of the lake. He did not leave the cabin again for two straight days. Between the ticks, the leeches, and the inevitable invasion of the mosquitoes, there simply wasn't enough blood in him to go around.

The towering Jack pines swayed in unison in the wind like concertgoers moving to the music. Jake walked heavily through the forest complete with long pants tucked into his well-used socks. It was his intense hunger that had driven him from the bugless confines of the cabin to the food-filled forest.

There was lots of space between the trees, so that a person could see quite a distance ahead. There were no crowded bushes or tangled branches, just the sturdy trunks shooting out of a plain of lush grass. There was enough space to feel the wind off the lake even though he was walking further and further away from it. The forest was usually full of hot, dead air and even the slightest air movement was a relief to Jake.

Over the winter, Jake's hair had grown past the nape of his neck, curling up at the ends and hiding his ears. His muscles in his back and shoulders were well defined over his otherwise scrawny arms from hours upon hours of chopping and carrying firewood, and moving and lifting heavy snow. Any baby fat that he had been carrying had long since vanished.

His hands were rough with cuts and calluses and his fingernails were worn down—not nearly as much as his grandfather's, but definitely getting there. The direct effects of hard work. The knuckles on both hands were scraped and scabbed over. His arms and legs were an array of cuts, scratches and bruises, daily reminders of his new life and prickly surroundings. They did not bother him anymore. The tumour was still the size of a golf ball, but the cancer was not spreading, not growing, and that was very good news indeed. It was lying dormant in there. Not shrinking, no, he is not that lucky, but lucky just the same. His energy levels were steady; the headaches had gone and not come back. He hadn't swallowed a pill since he had sunk them last year on Lampshine.

On this day Jake was doing what he had been doing almost daily since the snow melted: grouse hunting. Jake missed a lot of things that he had taken for granted back in the city, like playing football on Saturdays with his friends, and video games. He found that he missed simple things like salad dressing, band-aids, peanut butter cups, toilet paper and the drawer full of clean socks that his mother always stocked for him. But what he found that he missed most of all was the mind-numbingly simple task of picking up a phone and ordering a pizza.

When he was hungry and the pantry was empty back then all he had to do was hit speed-dial three on the Lucknow household phone and Pizza-4-U would come by twenty minutes later with a greasy, cheesy, overloaded Hawaiian Special for fifteen bucks and a free bottle of pop if he was lucky. The only thing that money was good for out here was starting fires.

Back home if money had been short he could always raid the fridge and munch on a variety of different snacks. Push-come-to-shove he was only a five-minute walk away from the corner store where he could pay a buck for a large bag of ketchup-flavoured potato chips.

In the bush, when his stomach rumbled, it called for some hunting and gathering action every single time, and it was wearing thin on his nerves. He was trying to learn to preserve and save food for later but he had developed a steady habit of devouring everything he had gotten in a matter of minutes.

Jake could gauge what kind of hunting day he was going to have by the colour of the sky. Today, it was a particular shade of greasy sheet metal: flat grey with wisps of black. It was not going to be a pleasant day. The grouse would stay in the brush cover since there was no reason to sun themselves in the open areas, which would have made it much easier for Jake to see them. It was also cooler and Jake didn't exactly have a full wardrobe to pick through. He had light clothes for the hot days, and heavy coverings for the winter, but he didn't have much in the in-between department—just an old hooded sweatshirt that was held together with not much more than a hope and a prayer.

Despite his low expectations he did manage to spot one spruce grouse sitting under a brush of red berries obliviously chomping away. Hardly believing his luck Jake scanned the ground and carefully selected a round shaped rock that fit perfectly in the palm of his hand. He rolled it around, testing its heft, and slowly moved forward.

The bird had its back to him and so far had not heard him. Jake tried to get close enough to take a decent shot at the prey but not close enough to spook away lunch. These birds usually let him get ridiculously close, under the false impression they were invisible even in the great wide open.

He stopped, controlled his breathing like he was firing a gun, cocked his arm and let the rock fly. Jake's line was dead on the money but the stone hit the dirt two feet in front of its target, skipped twice and hit the grouse right in its feathery rear end which prompted it to take off like a rocket into the forest.

Jake's shoulders slumped while his stomach blared its displeasure. He walked up to the berry bush and kicked the rock up the path. The berries were red and transparent enough that you could almost see through them. He picked a handful and carefully sampled one. His grandfather had told him to be very careful with what he ate from the forest floor, mushrooms or otherwise. But, this wasn't on the forest floor, and they obviously hadn't hurt the grouse.

The berry puckered the inside of his mouth, and he winced at its bitterness. If it was good enough for the birds it was good enough for him. His hungry stomach tightened slightly which Jake took for a sign of appetite and closed his eyes tight as he dumped the entire handful into his mouth. They reminded him of the sour candy he used to buy for a penny back in the city, in his old life.

He hopped around madly on one foot as his mouth instantly parched. He couldn't help but laugh and as he did some of the clear red juice streamed out either side of his mouth. "The bitterness jig!" he laughed out loud. He plucked another handful, his lips and fingers stained red and popped them in his mouth as the sun burned a hole through the thin clouds and threw light through the trees. Rejuvenated, he picked another palm-sized rock from the path—this one with a few more edges to hold onto—and continued through the forest.

About half an hour later he spotted a very large ruffed grouse that was fatter than a CFL football and the colour of deep mahogany. Jake licked his lips. The ruffies tasted a lot better than their pine needle-flavoured darker cousins. This bird had evidently spotted Jake as well as it had stopped dead in its tracks and tried to blend in with the background.

The jagged rock cut through the air like a major-league fastball, sailed well over the grouse's head, and carried on uninterrupted between two staggered tree trunks, and through a few leaves. Jake expected it to be swallowed silently by the moss-cushioned forest floor. Instead, he heard the rock bounce off something decidedly metallic with an acoustic twang. *Twang?* In the forest? Jake raised an eyebrow, something he had subconsciously picked up from his grandfather, and slowly made his way past the two trees and towards whatever his poorly aimed rock had smacked into.

The strange sound had made him momentarily forget both his hunger, and the bird, which was still doing its best statue impression right until Jake almost stepped on it. It exploded from the ground like a bomb of feathers, its wings booming noisily as it escaped to the top of the nearest tree. Jake dove for cover and cursed his carelessness just before he landed face first on the ground.

He waited until his heart returned to a normal pace before he picked himself up, and brushed pine needles and dirt off his shirt and forehead. He scanned the ground for more grouse grenades but didn't see anything. He tentatively proceeded forward. What he saw, right there in plain sight, made him stop dead in his tracks.

An airplane, more specifically a float plane, was mere metres away from him. This particular plane had not seen much flight time for quite a while. One float was completely missing, the nose and propeller was half buried in the ground and rust had formed like barnacles on the metal of the faded red and yellow fuselage. Moss covered the mostly collapsed windshield and the wings were cut in halves, no doubt sheared off by the thick trees trunks during the crash landing a very long time ago. The glass was mostly broken and the small windows that were still intact had a sickly yellow stain on them that prevented him from seeing inside.

After a long winter of seeing nothing but snow and ice the plane looked as out of place as a three-ring circus. Jake stared at it for a long time, afraid to take another step closer. Afraid and a little bit excited. He slowly and carefully walked around the entire perimeter of the plane. It was spooky.

Jake had stumbled upon what months of searching back in 1974 had not uncovered: a downed bush plane that was transporting supplies to a Northern prospecting camp. Jake shivered at the ghost-like scene. He realized that the pilot and passengers had likely not survived the crash and that they were probably still entombed in the small aircraft. He was hesitant, just as he was with everything he came across in the woods, but moved forward nonetheless. There might be something useful on board that he would be able to salvage.

The new afternoon sun had already baked the metal of the plane so that it was hot to the touch. Jake avoided the cockpit door, instead opting for the cargo. This proved to be a good idea as the door was hanging on by one rusted bolt and he could see inside the old plane. There was debris strewn about all over the place.

He tried to pull the door open but realized that the bottom part was getting caught on the ground. It wouldn't budge so he peeled the top half back like a tin of sardines. He shimmied his skinny frame into the suffocating stale air of the cargo area. He was inside.

Beads of sweat popped on his forehead without warning. The inside of the plane was like an oven and it was much smaller than Jake had imagined. Mercifully, there didn't appear to be any dead bodies in the cargo hold. This plane must have been a supply plane. *Somebody must have been flying it* his mind kept insisting. He pushed that thought to the back of his brain and looked around the chaos of the plane. He kept his head down, steering his search away from the cockpit opening.

There were mouldy blankets and old clothing scattered around the metal floor, mostly ravaged by mice. There was what looked like hundreds of tins of beans scattered around, the insides of which must have been cooked several times over by the hot sun. There was a crate of old brown bottles with faded labels, only a few of them broken. As Jake poked through the crate more carefully he realized that it was beer. The bottles had been carefully cushioned with newspaper and straw and seventeen of the twenty-four had somehow managed to survive the impact. He fished the broken glass out and pulled the crate to the middle of the floor. He had plans for the beer.

There were a few aged oil lamps that had been smashed beyond usefulness and a few empty barrels that were stamped

GAS and OIL that were now bone dry. It had been a miracle that they hadn't ignited. Over time, rust had eaten holes through the metal and the gas and oil had leaked out of the barrels, out of the plane, and leached into the soil. He made a mental note to mention the drums to his grandfather, as he may want to retrieve them for burn barrels.

He pulled a ratty looking backpack from the floor and emptied the contents. Mice-chewed maps and documents spilled out along with some petrified food and moth-infested clothes. He kicked the contents to the side and threw the pack on the crate of bottles.

Jake even found a shotgun, the barrel of which was twisted like a pretzel. The wooden stock was fractured and split. It would never be fired again and he left it where it was.

Jake, somewhat disappointed that he didn't find anything exotic like a haul of gold or a bag full of diamonds, pushed the crate of beer bottles out the opening in the cargo door and got ready to step out. He stopped and looked towards the front of the plane. Through the passage between the cargo hold and the cockpit, Jake could see that the pilot seat was indeed occupied — the back shoulder of a tattered leather jacket and a headset that was pulled over a very old brown cap was barely visible over the lip of the seat. Jake had to look at the pilot. It was the part of human nature that he could not fully understand. When ninety-five percent of your mind is saying to leave the plane, humans will invariably listen to the smaller, nagging five percent that says it couldn't hurt to look.

"Curiosity killed the cat," Jake mumbled under his breath as he stepped over the mice-eaten, moth-ridden clothing and took a relatively cautious position behind the co-pilot's seat, which was empty.

The pilot was nothing more than a perfect skeleton now. Its permanently grinning face stared at Jake through a pair of dusty mirrored sunglasses, which had slid halfway down his face as his nose had decomposed. Jake gasped. The only thing he could think of was what the last moments of this man's life must have been like: the feeling of falling through the sky like a rock. Jake wondered how much control he had at the end, if any. If he thought that he was going to make it. How terrifying it must have been and how instantly over his life had been.

Jake looked over the instrument panel whose dials were frozen in time and glass splintered into star-shaped cracks. The throttle was broken with the top half resting in the pilots lap, no doubt snapped in half during the impact. The radio hung uselessly between the seats and Jake could practically hear him screaming bloody murder into the handset as the plane went down.

That permanent smile was more than likely a scream frozen in time. Chills ran down his spine. Jake's eyes wandered back to the aviator glasses which would be very useful not only in the summer sun but for next winter as well. He had almost gone snow blind last winter. The dilemma in his head was that it seemed more than a little disrespectful to take a dead man's personal effects especially from his final resting place. Common sense won out over morals however, as he carefully plucked the glasses off the pilot's head and hung them on his shirt collar. The pilot would not be in danger of going snow blind. He briefly considered taking the leather jacket as well but quickly lost the gumption required to remove it. Instead, he turned and hurried towards the cargo door where he squeezed out back into the fresh outdoors.

It took more than two hours for Jake to push, pull, lug and drag the beer crate back to the cabin. It was the type of work that he didn't mind doing even though he was drenched in sweat by the time he set the old box down on the porch step. It became apparent very quickly that these were not like his father's beer bottles with the twist-off caps. These were the shorter, stubbier ancestors of the modern long neck version. The caps were *definitely* not twist-off as Jake burned a blistered ring in his palm to the point of drawing blood trying to remove them that way.

"Bottle opener. Add that to the shopping list." He grunted sarcastically. Beads of sweat stung his eyes, which pushed his frustration level over the top. He stormed down to the lake's edge and threw himself in the cold water. He sat on the sandy bottom and let himself cool off mentally and physically. He desperately wanted to get in those beer bottles.

He went back up the sandy path, careful not to stub his toes on the protruding tree roots, and pulled one of the stubbies from the case. He set the lip of the cap against the edge of the stair and held the bottle tightly from below. He gulped and braced himself for pain and then slammed the open palm of his other hand onto the cap. A chunk of wood from the stairs splintered from the force but in the process also blew the cap off the ancient bottle.

Jake smiled and ignored the angry red welt in the middle of his hand. Only sixteen more to go.

Seventeen bottles of beer were perched neatly on the partially replenished woodpile behind the cabin. The sun hit the brown glass and the golden liquid inside and made a kaleidoscope of beer light. Jake held up the first bottle and held it to his lips. It smelled sickly sweet and he took a small sip. He spat it out in a fine mist and gagged. Duly noted... beer was terrible, especially over thirty years past the expiration date.

He poured the stale skunky drink out with a steady tilt. He put the empty bottle back on the pile and proceeded to dump the rest out in a puddle on the grass. The puddle did not take long to attract some delirious sand flies. As long as they stayed in the pool of beer and away from his bare ankles, Jake did not mind. When he was finished he kicked sand over the beer to avoid accidentally luring any bears to the cabin.

With all the bottles empty Jake packed them back into the crate and headed back towards the water. He washed out each bottle carefully and brought them back to the porch where he set them on the deck to dry out.

His work half done, he stretched out on the porch chair and fell fast asleep.

While Jake was snoozing in the mid-day sun, the Moonstone wolf pack was in major distress. The wolves, as an entire pack, used to hunt and eat a deer every week or so. Now, they ate one daily—each of them! At their current pace they would need to look elsewhere for food. Their stomachs had become bottomless black pits of hunger.

The alpha male was still the unquestioned leader of the polluted pack. His beautiful black coat had been bleached white, which seemed to terrify the rest of them and fear was always an important ingredient in maintaining leadership. Every day when the sun rose and again before it fell, he inspected the pack for weakness or defects. The horde was much more efficient as one and if one of the animals so much as developed a limp it would be dispatched immediately.

Once in a while, in their delirium, one of the other males would nip or take a swipe at their pale leader, as if to probe for *his* flaws. That wolf would quickly regret the assessment, and end up missing chunks of flesh from his hide because of it.

Right now they were hunting again and acting as one very well oiled killing machine. Their quarry was the large buck that stood still but heaved in exhaustion on the bare rock in the middle of a sparsely treed forest.

Blood and adrenaline coursed through the deer's body. The wolves had chased him for twenty miles and he could go no further. He had been blessed with blazing speed but not so much endurance. Nonetheless, he usually had no trouble outrunning the pack.

Even the joaquin had not bothered the buck this much. The big cat had developed a taste for humans over time mainly because they were so much slower and easier to catch than any other wild animals. As it aged, it became lazy and as more miners or railway men or hydro linemen entered the Gem Lakes, the more it was able to feast with ease.

The wolves were getting bigger and faster. The deer would soon become few and far between.

Jake wrote until his hand cramped and he couldn't physically hold the tiny nub of a pencil anymore. He had found the old carpenter's pencil in an even older tin in the cabin's shelving and he wasn't sure how much more he could get out of it. His blistered fingertips were worn numb and covered in lead. He had been painstakingly writing the same message, word-for-word, on seventeen pieces of birch bark and rolling the natural paper into tight scrolls. He tied each one delicately with the carefully sliced blade of a cattail stalk. It was, at first, a very difficult letter to put together. He didn't want to come across as corny or too dramatic. He just wanted it to be real.

He had to make sure that his family wasn't mad at him or thought that *he* was mad at them. He was worried about that. In the end, he just wrote how he felt at that moment, and let the words flow from the pencil to the page—as much as they could flow from the stubby pencil, anyway. He very carefully and meticulously copied each and every word and letter, making sure not to change so much as a punctuation mark. He had no way of knowing which of the bottles, if any, they would find. He wanted to know for sure which words they were going to read. Jake also hoped that *all* the bottles didn't land on the dock or he'd look like an idiot.

Jake had always had a very sneaking suspicion that some of his grandfather's "hunting" trips were instead rendezvous with his dad somewhere on the outskirts of the Gem Lakes.

Those suspect trips were always a little longer than usual and he had a habit of coming back with less meat than usual—maybe a token grouse or a rabbit that he had killed on the last lake back to avert questions.

The main clue that Rusty was meeting his own son was that days after the trip new socks would mysteriously appear in the bottom of his trunk; new candles would show up in the tin above the table; somehow, the box of wooden matches never seemed to run out, the same with the small drum of kerosene that was seemingly bottomless: all these small things that his grandfather would give dodgy answers to.

Rusty Lucknow knew the Gem Lakes better than anyone. He knew where the bears were likely to be at any given time. He knew which rocks were loose and which were safe to step on. He knew how to avoid trouble and to fade away into the scenery even if he chanced upon it. The old man had a lifetime of experience in these parts and could move freely without worrying about the unknown. In the Gem Lakes, it was the unknown that could kill you.

It had crossed his mind that he could simply call his grandfather's bluff and ask to come along or at least send a letter along with him but Rusty wasn't keen on keeping the connection to Lampshine Lake open. At least for now.

It's like an open wound for Criss' sake! Let it heal a little will ya? Let it scab over!

When he scrawled his name on the bottom of the last letter, he stretched his tortured hand and winced. He popped a scroll in each of the bottles and then placed all seventeen caps back on the tops. Some were more damaged than others but Jake managed to pinch all of them back in place with the help of a very old pair of needle-nosed pliers that Jake's grandfather kept in his fishing gear. As a final touch he lined them all up on the top stair and inspected them like a general would his soldiers. One to seventeen. They were ready.

Rusty Lucknow passed by The Creek With No Name just as Jake was gently tossing bottle number fifteen into the quick-moving current. He stood in complete disbelief as he tried to convince himself that he was not watching his own flesh and blood throwing beer into the creek. He could barely get the words out as he came up behind his grandson. "Are my eyes playin' tricks on me or am I seein' you throw *beer* into that there rushin' water?"

Jake, startled at first, caught number fifteen in mid-toss. "Oh hey, Gramps." He was just starting to get used to calling Rusty gramps or grandpa. "Yeah, you'll never believe what I found in the forest. A plane! I got these beer bottles and some other stuff too. I saw the pilot ... but ... but, well, other than that it was really cool."

Rusty held his hand up to put a stop to the rambling. "Am I seeing you *throw beer* into that there rushin' water," he repeated incredulously. He moved forward and plucked the bottle out of Jake's hand. It was his brand ... well, it had been, many, many years ago. He didn't think they even made that kind anymore. Sipping cold brews in the hot sun, feet dangling in the lake off the dock after a good afternoon's work, letting summer afternoons dissolve away into summer evenings. Memories.

"What's inside?" It sure wasn't beer.

"Uh, nothing special."

"They were full?"

"They were. I poured them out." Jake took the bottle back and flicked it into the creek. In moments, it was out of sight, being carried away effortlessly by the current.

"You poured them out—" He winced at every syllable.

Jake looked at his grandfather quizzically. He was sure acting strange.

The last two bottles followed the fifteenth and the race was on.

Rusty rubbed his eyes and shook off the shock, "Listen, I have to go on a little trip. You're going to be by yourself for a while. Can you handle it?"

"How long is a while?"

"Four or five days, weather depending I'll be leaving by week's end."

The scene from that spring on the not-so-frozen lake was still fresh in both their minds. This would be Rusty's first extended trip since that night.

"I can handle it." *I won't do anything stupid this time* is what they both heard.

Rusty needed to check on his trapline and repair and replace some of the older ones. He had neglected them a little bit this year because of Jake, but they couldn't go on much longer without some meat in their diet. Jake was losing weight and the old man had started to worry about him. He had some fish drying in racks, had crushed some acorns into flour for bannock and had picked some cattail stalks for frying earlier this morning. He would take a minimal amount for himself on his travels and leave the rest for Jake.

The cramps started just after the first evening stars were flickering on the canvas of night sky. At first, they didn't seem too bad, almost like the stitch in your side that you get if you run too fast for too long. Then a gurgling and a minor discomfort that made him shift from side to side and soon it felt like there was a smouldering piece of coal sitting in the pit of his stomach.

Finally, an hour later Jake was doubled-over by the campfire, a cold sweat covered his body and he was shivering uncontrollably. His hair was plastered to his forehead in long, wet strands.

"Red berries… boy, if it wasn't a raspberry and it was red I don't know what you were thinkin' eatin' it." Rusty was actually somewhat relieved. He had been concerned about Bloodbite which some of the mosquitoes around the Gem Lakes carried. It was a poison blood that ran up your spine, pushing spinal fluid to the base of the brain and literally drowning it.

"C-c-c-ranberry?"

"You can't see through no cranberry, boy."

"W-well the grouse was eating them!"

"Oh Lord. Boy, do you know why those fool birds sit on the gravel paths all day? It ain't to get a suntan! They *eat* the gravel boy! It helps them digest those bitter berries that you chowed on. You didn't eat no rocks today—didya boy?"

Right now, Jake was wishing he had eaten a garden full of rocks. He mentioned the bitterness jig to his grandfather who then furrowed his brow. "You'll be doing a different kind of jig in a few hours...one you'll be dancin' to all night."

Rusty Lucknow did not lie. Jake spent the entire night in the bush a body's length away from the biffy. He was completely unaware of the blackness or the night sounds or the bugs or anything else but the terrible pain in his belly. He had murdered his stomach—of that much he was sure.

He woke up with his grandfather shaking him. He was face down on the path with pine needles and dirt pasted to one side of his face. The other side was so peppered with mosquito bites it looked like he had taken a load of birdshot to the face. His skin felt cool and clammy but the pain in his gut was mercifully missing. It was getting light outside. "I think you purged the poison, boy. Let's get you to the cabin—you'll need some good rest."

After three straight days of drinking nothing but boiled lake water and tea steeped from spruce needles and lying wrapped in a blanket in bed, Jake's stomach had once again forced him up out of the cabin and back in the saddle of the horse that had bucked him: bird hunting.

Today however, was sunny and clear and he felt recharged with the sun's rays on the back of his neck. He walked briskly through the forest following a twisting deer path and tried to get the blood flowing through his wobbly legs. His first stop was the exact spot where he had launched the beer bottles in the Creek With No Name. He had been having several bad dreams about finding them all hung up on a sand bar somewhere and wanted peace of mind that they all at least left the starting gate. The coast was clear for as far as Jake could follow the creek he didn't spot one bottle caught in the rocks or logs that littered the water. *Maybe they have a chance after all* he thought to himself.

Maybe the bottles did have a chance. The crow was enthralled at this possibility. He watched as all seventeen bottles left the Creek With No Name intact and unencumbered. But, that was as far as most of them would get. You see, the Creek With No Name wound through the forest and dumped into a mini-lake, also with no name, which had a mini-waterfall at the other end. Bottles one through six did not make it down said waterfall: five of them smashed to pieces on the rocks and the sixth hopelessly lodged in between two logs that hadn't stirred in over a dozen years.

The remaining eleven navigated the rocks and rapids and spilled safely into a calm pool that would need the wind to pick up before they moved any farther.

Three majestic poplars stood guard near the edge of the water. They were unusually tall and swayed dramatically in even the slightest breeze. Rusty was sharpening a knife on the steps. His loaded pack sat beside him. He had delayed his departure due to Jake's sickness. He noticed Jake, on the other side of the pack, watching the enormous trees.

"They're beauties," Rusty commented.

"They'll come down and kill us one day. Crush us like bugs."

"They're old."

"They're rotten."

"They're heavy."

"They're heavy all right," Jake agreed. "Cabin Killers." The problem with poplars, as was commonly known, was that they could rot anywhere up their trunks making it unpredictable as to when and where they would snap off. Their sheer weight and density made them dangerous. Their proximity to the cabin made them treacherous.

The old man looked up at the flickering leaves of the ancient trees and frowned. It was as if Jake was insulting his friends.

"All right. It's time I go. You remember the rules?"

Jake looked up, doing his best to disguise his nervousness. "Stick close to the cabin. Stay inside after dusk. Don't eat all the food."

"Ah hah then," Rusty picked up the pack and swung it easily over his shoulder. He rubbed Jake's hair, something he had never done. "And if I don't come back for some reason?"

Jake hesitated. "Don't come looking for you."

"Do not come lookin' for me. If I ain't back then there's a reason that you don't need to go find."

The nights that Rusty was gone were much different for Jake than the ones when they shared the cabin. The things that go bump in the night seemed to bump just a little louder when he was alone. Mice that scurried around the wooden floor seemed like ferocious sewer rats. The slightest wind sounded like the mournful groans of some animal that wanted badly to break down the cabin door. It took him hours longer to fall asleep without the protective shield of his grandfather across the room. It wasn't too bad in the winter when the only thing moving in the forest was snow. In the summer, when the forest came alive at night it was a different story.

Jake would have preferred to start a roaring fire and fall asleep to the sound of it crackling away but it was already warm in the room and the heat from the fire would push it past bearable.

He finally fell asleep, as usual, when he ran out of terrible things to imagine just outside the door. The one advantage to keeping himself up late was that he could usually sleep straight through until morning—on most nights.

In the middle of this night, however, Jake snapped awake. He lay on his side in the small cot and listened. Sometimes he would wake up to the occasional mouse that scrambled over his body or the sound of an ember rattling around the fireplace. After a minute or two of listening he could not hear the telltale squeak of a mouse. He had not made a fire in the fireplace in over two weeks.

His back was to the door and window and Jake could not force himself to turn around to face them. He wondered if an animal had knocked open the door somehow and was now staring at him from the middle of the floor. He could not overcome the overpowering feeling that somebody or something was watching him. Soon, his imagination ran away into the absurd and he started thinking about alien spaceships that might be hovering above the roof at this very moment or a large hairy Sasquatch standing in the frame of the door. He counted to three in his head and flipped over, half expecting to scream but mostly expecting to see nothing but an empty room.

There was a face in the window. Jake's scream caught somewhere between his lungs and his larynx and his eyes bulged in fear. The face seemed to be surprised as well. It was the face of a woman and she put her hand to the window before fading backwards into the darkness.

Jake had tried to push the image of the face in the window out of his mind and had almost convinced himself that he had dreamt the entire thing but nonetheless found it was the first thing that tumbled out of his mouth when his grandfather came back from his traplines.

"A woman?" he frowned. He rested the old shotgun he still carried on the tree stump beside him. The gun made Jake nervous. Since the joaquin had been killed last summer the shotgun had hung ornamentally above the door in the cabin. Something in the woods lately had been making his grandfather nervous and the gun had come down, even though it still had no ammo. His grandfather thought the animals around the Gem Lakes were intelligent enough to remember when the gun did work and at least be wary of it. Most of them were.

"Yeah, staring in like she was looking for someone."

"Sure ya weren't dreamin'?"

Jake was still not completely sure that he hadn't dreamt the entire thing but he didn't usually remember his dreams. "I don't think so ... it kinda looked like a ghost."

The old man was quiet for a moment then sat down on the bottom step of the porch and ground his heel into the sandy dirt. He removed his cap and swatted mindlessly at some no-see-ums.

"Willow witch."

"What's that?"

Jake swore he saw the old man flinch before he spoke; like he didn't know the whole story or worse, he *did* know, but just didn't like telling it.

"Back in the day thousands of folks were crawling all over this country looking for another Klondike. They found in short order that the gold around here wasn't just lying around in shallow rivers. No sir, it takes a helluva lot of effort to pull it out of the ground around here. The earth is a little heartier in this country, eh?

"The folks who made it the furthest never made it past Cemetery Lake, about twenty miles north of here. They named it such because there are over thirty graves sunk around that place. They say that there's enough skeletons underneath that water to lay a track of bone from there to Boston."

"How did so many people die?" Jake asked, eyes wide.

"It was a matter of unpreparedness more than anything else. Not enough food, not enough clothing, not enough brains.

"Years and years and years ago, before my time even, two well-to-do couples from California hired an old prospector to take them into the Gem Lakes range, looking for precious metals or gemstones, maybe even a vein of gold. They had missed the boat to the Yukon. When they got here they didn't know a moose from a muskrat. The ladies wore fur coats. Well winter came up on them in a Gawdawful hurry and the prospector bailed out, told them that to go on was suicide. They kept pushin' bush, fur coats and all and soon it was only the one husband and wife, starving and frozen, taking the clothes right off the corpses of the other two for warmth. They took to eating their huskies and skinning the coats for hats. Sounds cruel but exposure is a terrible way to die. Those dogs got mercy I can guarantee you that.

"Soon the husband was delirious with hypothermia and the wife set out by herself in a blizzard to get help. Pushed her way into the mining camp with that fancy mink coat keeping her alive. By the time a search party made it back to the tent, the husband was dead, frozen solid in the same position she had left him in.

"What happened?"

"She went berserk and tore away from the mining party, disappeared into the bush. Nobody ever saw her again, dead or alive. She disappeared into the willows and never came out the other side."

"Maybe the joaquin got her."

Rusty Lucknow shrugged. "Maybe," he said. "They say that she's like the miners; that because she never stops walking, never stops trying to get out, that she didn't take the time to die."

Jake shivered and stole a glance over his shoulder.

"I thought I saw her before ... once," the old man admitted.

"When?"

"Years ago ... ages ago, '60? 61? I was track'n a moose in the fall for the winter's meat and I stepped on an old steel jaw trap that some fool had left unchecked and forgotten about. Damn near snapped my leg off at the shin. I broke it good anyway. Passed out. The thing was fester'n with rust and dirt and it was a no good situation that's for sure.

"I wasn't able to move for a while, couldn't open the jaws, kept passing in and out 'cause of the pain. I saw the woman in the middle of the night, thought it was the angel of mercy coming to escort me to the pearly gates. Thought I was going delirious... beautiful woman in the middle of nowhere."

"What happened?"

"Don't know. I woke up the next morning and the trap was open."

"Your leg was healed?"

"No. Still snapped like a twig. I had to drag my sorry butt out a foot at a time through the bush, around the lakes, up the ballast and onto the Lampshine track. Waved down a freighter."

Jake digested all of this. "Maybe you somehow opened the trap in the night? You know, adrenaline or something?"

"Maybe."

There was silence for a minute. Then Rusty got to his feet and yawned. "Listen, I tracked a small herd of caribou a bit past Moonstone, headed south. That's easy meat for a season. I'll be leavin' at first light."

The crow saw through his black eyes that Jake thought his grandfather had slipped over the deep end with his story of the willow witch, for he had never heard of creatures such as that in his learnings through school or books or motion pictures for that matter. Jake had seen with his very own eyes, and yet had dismissed it as a dream. This was the case with humans as they had rarely ventured as deep into the forest as they were congregated in now. Sure, a few of them would wander into the very back of their cottage lots and look for berries or property lines or even stealthy harvest an over-sized Jack pine from what was technically their neighbours lot, but they had *never* beaten the bush this deep, nor would they ever. Most men in the civilized world lacked the spine for such a journey and as humans always did, they were skeptical of things that they had not laid their own eyes on.

Rusty sat patiently behind the nest of bulrushes under the tree that used to have the Opal Portage marker nailed to it. There had been no herd of caribou; there never had been this far south. It was just a handy excuse.

He chewed on a blade of grass until he noticed the familiar speck of a canoe coming towards him from the opposite side of Timber Wolf Lake, just south of the Gem Lakes Range.

The silhouette of the lone paddler grew larger with each stroke, and soon, Bob Lucknow manoeuvred the canoe into the bulrushes. Rusty could make out a crooked, nervous smile through the low light of dusk.

A voice came softly through dusk, "Dad?"

Rusty, known to his son and others outside of the Gem Lakes as Gordon Lucknow, waved and picked himself up off the ground. This was not going to be their usual small talk.

Gordon grabbed the front of the canoe and pulled it to shore. He shook hands heartily with his son and they gave each other a powerful one-armed hug.

"How's Susan? How's Claire?"

"Good, good. Claire's off to the East Coast. And Sue, well, she's hanging in there. This is all a lot to digest. She's having trouble accepting it."

Gordon nodded gravely.

Bob looked uncomfortable. "How's the weather been this year?"

The father raised an eyebrow at the son. "Jake's been fine ... real fine actually."

The considerable weight of an unknown winter was lifted off Bob's back. He breathed a deep lungful of relief. "The tumour?"

"What tumour?" Gordon shrugged. Father and son shared a knowing smile, like they were both in on a cosmic-sized inside joke.

Rusty Lucknow could have taken a much more direct route home, straight through the still bloated creeks that lined the forest rock, but he took the longer way, as he always did: the way that took him along the north side of Moonstone Lake; the way that led past Chipper's old hut and now, in the last year, his grave. It was time to pay respects to an old friend.

Chipper Prefontaine had, of course, been the first man to trap in the Gem Lake Range. Rusty could remember the day he first joined him in the back lakes, when he and Chipper had struck up an easy friendship while the elder Lucknow was building the cottage his son's family now inhabited.

Chipper would cut cords of wood in exchange for pipe tobacco, or fresh water, or coffee. Gordon, as he was still known back then, had always thought the trapper to be a little on the eccentric side but always seemed to be a man who embraced the life he was living. Then life had handed Gordon a big fat lump of coal. It was his unusual friend that had saved him from his own self-pity and shown him that life was too short to pout about the value of the hand that was dealt to him. At least, the old trapper had pointed out, he was still in the game. He was right. Gordon left his old life behind, and took on the name of his hair color.

Then, out of nowhere, Jake and Claire, his own grand-kids had shown up, and Rusty had spent and entire winter trying to drive that same realization of life into his grandson's thick skull: play the hand dealt. It was as simple as that.

The leather boot laces had shrunk around the rusted re-bar so that the makeshift grave marker was actually in better shape than Rusty had left it in the summer. The site was not ideal, Rusty would have loved to have given Chipper a view of one of the many lakes that he had lived near and loved, but finding a spot in this granite covered land to sink a grave, well, the choices were limited. Even when the rock wasn't visible to the eye it was never far beneath the surface. It was the same reason that most of the cottagers on Lampshine Lake had outhouses that weren't even within throwing distance of their cabins. Some people joked that they needed to pack a lunch anytime they needed to make the trip.

Nonetheless, Rusty had managed to find a very nice spot in the lush green grass, under the massive umbrella of a tree.

He got down on one knee and made the sign of the cross. "In the name if the father, the son and the holy-trapper...," he mumbled quickly. He spent the next ten minutes down on the same knee, remembering.

The mud hut had wintered well. Rusty had left some of Chipper's books and a few little trinkets on the wood shelves but it was otherwise empty. The wooden door had shifted slightly in the cold and was just ever so slightly stubborn to pull open. When it did it made the sound of a champagne cork popping and the air inside smelled stale and strongly of earth. There were half a dozen mice lying dead as doornails on the cold floor. They had not wintered as well. Rusty plucked them up one by one and tossed them on the rock outside. The crows would take them by the time he left.

He remembered fondly the times that they spend in the hut with only the stub of a candle to warm the place and a well-worn pack of playing cards. Countless cribbage games on the old antler board. He sparked up a small fire in the concaved pit and spent the night.

Rusty did not see the wolf standing directly in front of him. Not at first. Leaving the darkness of the hut, the blinding light of the sun forced his eyes into squinted slits. He slowly swallowed two mouthfuls of morning mugginess and only after shading his eyes with his hand did he see that he was not alone.

There were two other wolves on either side of the first, both about twenty feet away. They looked like they were part of the Moonstone pack but bigger—like their muscles and bones had grown but their hides had stayed the same and now seemed grotesquely stretched over their frames.

Rusty eyed the biggest one carefully. He was long and lithe and his hair was pure white. The animal's fur had been shocked colorless right down to the hair follicles. His eyes shone impossibly blue and his ears were pinned back on his head; his lips curled back in aggression.

The others would not react until their leader did but Rusty was not quite sure what they wanted in the first place. The Moonstone pack had always been very peaceful and Rusty had always taken great care to make sure not to set snares in their territory. He wondered if they were sick with mange but they sure didn't look like they had been hurting for food.

The hair on the back of the ghostly leader was raised and that made the hair on the nape of Rusty's neck do the same. He slowly picked up the empty shotgun that he had left leaning against the hut. He sorely wished he had more shells. Rusty had never shot at the wolves and they didn't know to fear it. He would have to settle this the old-fashioned way.

After losing his right hand, his left arm had developed into twice the size. He had learned to be more than capable defending himself with one arm. He could get more force behind his swing than most men with two.

A low whine escaped the throat of one of the wolves and the two on either side closed in. The leader pulled back his lips to reveal fangs the size of steak knives. They had grown so quickly that they had cut into the fleshy gums of the animal, obviously irritating him. His engorged clown-like tongue was slicked with blood from the wounds, hanging out of his mouth with anticipation.

These wolves were indeed sick, but it was not with mange.

The white one took a step backwards and howled so sharply that Rusty felt the sound waves pierce his body and freeze his lungs. The other two wolves bolted towards him in streaks of fangs and fur. Rusty judged the one on his left to be arriving quicker and he brought the sturdy but empty shotgun down hard on the charging wolf's sensitive snout. That one yelped and shirked away in pain. Just as quickly, he swung back hard and low to his right and caught the second wolf in mid-air, his gaping mouth and gnashing teeth on perfect line for the soft flesh of Rusty's exposed throat. The shotgun made crunching contact with the front right leg of the would-be throat-ripper. The wolf deflected sideways, catching only enough of the old bushman to knock him down. That wolf tried to pick himself up, but collapsed and crashed on the ground with a heavy thump, his leg useless and broken.

Still on his back, Rusty, for the first time noticed three more wolves directly above him, drooling and ready to pounce from the top of the mud hut. The first wolf that had taken the shot on the nose had recovered and was looming over him with the look of crazed rage. With foam flecked lips his eyes rolled back in his head as he snarled and snapped above him. The pale leader sauntered up by Rusty's feet, where the gun lay, having been knocked out of his good hand and stepped on the weapon with monster paws.

Rusty Lucknow lived another forty-five seconds, even managing to get a pretty good strangle hold on one of his attackers before the wolves pulled him apart limb by limb, impartial about good hand and bad. When the ravenous animals were finished, their muzzles dripping in crimson, they turned their attention to their ailing pack mate. He was shuffling away from the rest of the pack, knowing that with his snapped leg bone he had immediately become the weak link. The other five were on him in no time, and soon the injured wolf's spilled blood ran together with Rusty's in tiny red rivers, pooling in the concaved fire pit and on the fresh spring grass like morbid morning dew.

The red dawn melted Jake's built-up courage like a chocolate bar left on the car dash too long on a summer afternoon. The outside package looked the same but inside, slowly but surely, the chocolate or the bravery, whatever the case may be, was nothing more than a soft, gooey mess.

The wolves had started their frenzied howling two hours ago, and their pitch had only gotten more panicked as the early morning sky turned from vibrant blue to bright pink to blood red. The wolves were close, Jake figured a couple of miles at most, but did not seem to be moving either towards or away from him.

Bob stopped the axe in mid-swing. He was working on his beloved woodpile, which was divided neatly into stacks of Jack pine, birch, spruce and kindling. They were set out on the rock, which provided excellent drying when the sun was out.

His morning coffee sat half-drunk on an old oil drum.

He could not remember the last time that he had heard wolves during the day. Ten years? Twenty? Never? He wondered if they had come to the end of a successful hunt. He knew that they could pick up the scent of a wounded deer or moose from miles away and were excellent hunters. The thought crossed his mind that he had not seen a deer yet this year, not even the one that had frequented the woodpile over the years.

He looked back through a clearing in the woods towards the yellow cabin and noticed his wife standing in the half-open door, frowning. She had heard the wolves as well.

The old crow could tell that these wolves were not healthy. The dark gunk that they ingested from the joaquin infected their bodies, minds and souls.

He hopped across a Jack pine branch. Perhaps the ancient bird had become too attached to this man of the bush but there was most definitely a profound emptiness now—a void that felt a little too human for his liking. It made the bird feel that he may have crossed the line from observer to…something else, even though that cannot be. This could also be the reason that the old bird had not checked on Jake's precious beer bottles lately. The last time he had tracked them, bottle number seven had been sucked down a whirlpool and had not yet resurfaced, which was at least a better fate than bottle number eight whose cap had come loose on Ruby Lake and was now stuck upside down in the sandy bottom for all eternity, seven hundred feet below the surface.

When the crow first met Jake the boy had been living on borrowed time with his brain tumour. When Jake plummeted through the ice back in early spring the crow was concerned that the boy's life might be tragically taken before his due time once again. Now it would not be long—in fact, as soon as the wind blew in from the north—until these bloodthirsty wolves caught the scent of another Lucknow. The crow wondered if it would have been better for Jake just to catch the bus to the pearly gates the first time that it came for him, rather than face the terror that awaited him in the next few days and weeks.

He skittered nervously from branch to branch and lifted off towards the boy.

The figure slipped out of the dark shadows of the forest and into the open meadow as easily and naturally as sunlight falling across still morning water. The man marched steadily and with purpose towards the small cabin with a pack strapped to his back and a shotgun slung over his shoulder, the barrel of which was pointed straight up to heaven.

He paused only briefly at the bottom of the wooden stairs that he himself had helped build and made the long journey up the three split logs. What he had to do was difficult enough. Who he had to do it to was going to make it brutal.

He rapped his knobby knuckles on the door and slipped the old leather gun strap off his shoulder and gripped the weapon tightly in both hands.

The man's weather beaten face was dark from the sun and wind, and tiny particles of dirt clung to his skin, forming a thin mask that was almost indistinguishable from his whiskered jaw-line. He looked exhausted. There were two light lines on his face, thin and barely visible but there just the same, from both eyes down to his cheeks. The Mad Trapper of Lampshine Lake had been crying. He had dried his eyes but the stains remained as conclusive evidence.

A wave of nausea passed through Jake from tip to toe. Then he saw his grandfather's shotgun clutched in the trapper's hand.

"No—"

The trapper suddenly looked like the saddest creature on the face of the earth. He reached out his hand, offering the shotgun to Jake.

Jake looked away, furiously blinking away a sudden stream of his own tears.

"No, no no …."

The trapper said nothing but kept his hand steady.

The sun, a blob of orange, sat just above the horizon like a perfect egg yolk. It cast a light of fire over the morning water that held Jake in a silent spell for an entire hour. He had not eaten in two days and his neglected stomach would not allow him to sleep. His eyes were burned dry of moisture, although he was not sure whether that was from lack of rest or from crying so much that his tear ducts had simply run out of tears. It was one thing to be alone in the forest to hunt or fish, but it was quite another to be *really* alone. As in forever.

In the days following his grandfather's death Jake surrounded himself in a cocoon of silence. He stayed on the porch through good weather and bad and wondered how his seemingly bulletproof grandfather could have been killed. Jake worried very much that he hadn't learned enough from him—hadn't paid attention as much as he should have. He wondered if he should leave the Gem Lakes and tell his family but how could he? For years they assumed he was dead anyway—except for his dad who kept it a closely guarded secret. Claire had met him, and it was very likely that his mom knew the truth by now. What good did it do to tell them of his death? Especially when the trip was so dangerous. Especially if it meant he would have to leave the Gem Lakes. What would happen to him?

The trapper was shaken as well, much more than he would ever admit to. As a trapper it was his business to know animals: how they moved, why they moved and where they moved. As a man with over eighty years experience in the bush he was disappointed that he hadn't seen this coming. There was something wrong. The wolves had never been an aggressive pack.

He had a feeling that if he went back to where his friend had dumped the joaquin's body that he would find nothing, and finding nothing would explain everything.

Gordon "Rusty" Lucknow's funeral was sparsely attended but that probably goes without saying. The only other mourner present, other than the Mad Trapper, Jake, and an oversized but downtrodden crow, was a Whiskey Jack who sat perched on Chipper Prefontaine's steel cross next to the fresh one that the trapper had made, tied neatly together with Rusty's old boot laces. The Whiskey Jack sat still, very unlike the usually hyperactive bird, and cast a steady glance at the freshly turned earth. It looked like it was officiating the service but more than likely it was just looking for worms.

Jake was very thankful that the Mad Trapper had buried his grandfather's remains beforehand, very grateful that he had laid him in the ground already. He shivered as he remembered the horrible howling of the wolves that day and he now knew what they had been up to. It must have been a terrible thing for the trapper to see his best (only?) friend in the aftermath of that bloody battle. Jake knew that it had been vicious because they had had to pass the mud hut to get to the grave and he had made a point of trying to ignore the dark shadows of blood that were still stained on the rock. A flock of crows cawed loudly as they had approached, and then took off into the nearby trees when they had gotten too close. They had been picking at the sticky granite, and would no doubt continue when the funeral procession carried on. Flock was the wrong word though. *What was it again?* His grandfather had mentioned once. *Murder, that was it, a murder of crows.* Jake glanced up at the big scavengers, their beady black eyes reflecting nothing but pure hatred at the two humans that had interrupted their meal. *A murder of crows... well nothing could be more appropriate*, Jake thought to himself, as they had moved towards what could now be officially declared as the Gem Lakes Cemetery.

Six weeks rolled by and Jake did not leave the Lake of the Clouds. Instead, he was mired in a black pit of loneliness that seemed completely bottomless. Jake's sense of invincibility and safety that he had lost with the tumour, and then regained back here, had vanished again. He found that it cut more deeply the second time around.

The trapper had not stayed, sensing that Jake would need to be alone for a while. He did not go far however, and left Jake hunks of meat or fish every three days. The trapper slept across the lake in an overturned canoe. It was not the most comfortable spot he had ever taken camp but not the least either. Besides, it offered good protection against wolves, among other things.

Back at Lampshine Lake, summer carried on with the Lucknows oblivious to the goings on in the forest behind them. Bob continued to tie flies and putter around the cabin. He found it difficult to go fishing now that Jake was no longer there but he was easing his way back into it. Susan had taken up building patio furniture out of branches from a new book she had been given for Mother's Day by Claire. It had arrived in the mail the day before opening weekend.

Susan waged a daily war in her head regarding her son— whether it was exhilaration in allowing for the possibility that he was alive, or the utter devastation in imagining him not so. Sometimes in her mind she saw him making bow and arrows out of tree branches and having the time of his life and other times she saw piles and piles of bleached bones not given the proper burial or closure that she desperately needed. Either vision burned her in different ways.

In the meantime, the Moonstone wolf pack was taking a serious toll on the Gem Lake ecosystem. The deer population had plummeted. The crowded moose population had slipped off the charts and the bobcats, rabbits and fox had all taken a hit as well. The wolves were covering 150 miles a day and the more calories they burned they more they needed to consume. Mother Nature had not intended for the top of the forest food chain to be so prolific.

The forest was crashing.

The fresh smell of rain filled Jake's nostrils, and cleared his groggy head in an instant. It wasn't raining yet but it was coming. It was odd how a person could *smell* rain, Jake mused. How they could know it was coming; how it was in the air. A storm was brewing in the west and it looked to be a good one. Thunderheads were towering above a tin metal sky, with dark wisps swirling around the base at an alarming pace. Jake judged it to be a few hours away. He could see great forks of lighting leaving jagged scars across the sky and then hear the dull rumble of thunder following about eight seconds later. A mile for every second, that's what Rusty had told him. Yes, it was a few hours away still.

The storm that Jake had expected never made it as far as Lake of the Clouds. The wind changed course unexpectedly and blew the bruising thunderstorm back further west, towards the dry farmers fields that stretched all the way back to the city limits. The farmers could no doubt use the precipitation.

The air was still and humid, the smell of rain had been replaced by a stickiness that Jake was avoiding by dozing in the shade of the porch chair.

The crow shifted along the cord of an old clothesline that hung from the back corner of the cabin to a tall Jack pine. He was bored.

In the lowest depth of his loneliness Jake had opened the door one evening after a sparse dinner of perch only to almost step on an albino fox that was just about the size of a dog. It was just sitting there, staring at the door. His tongue was lolling out of its mouth, drawn by the smell of his fish dinner. With the white fur and the mischievous eyes, the thought flashed through Jake's mind that this animal might make a good pet for him: a good and decent companion. It soon became clear to the fox that Jake had not left even a morsel for him to chew on and it waited until Jake tried to pet it and then snapped at his hand, taking scallop-sized chunks of flesh from his knuckles. The wily animal showed up the next night as well but a scorned Jake met him at the threshold with a cast-iron pan to the face. The concussed fox never ventured to Jake's door again.

Three pelicans sat patiently on the peak of a lonely rock in the middle of an unnamed lake. They looked like they were dozing off in the afternoon sun, but were actually hunting. If a fish happened by that particular rock it was as good as lunch. The pelicans could hold three gallons of water (twice the capacity of their stomachs) in their impressive pouches. Normally, a pelican was bigger than an average sized bald eagle, with a wingspan of over nine-feet. These ones however were equipped with an eleven-foot span.

The pelicans were not the only birds hunting on this day, on this particular lake. A majestic golden eagle was perched unnoticed on a bare tree limb high above, as a slight breeze ruffled the namesake gold tinged feathers at the nape of her neck. She was larger than both a bald eagle and the pelicans despite what that armchair bird book might tell you. She had lived on this lake for over ten years where she'd made substantial additions to her massive nest each year. The nest would eventually fall down from its present location on a nearby treetop either from its own weight or a particularly rough snowstorm but for now it was an admirable fortress.

She watched the pelicans with seemingly mild interest for a while and then, suddenly and soundlessly, lifted off the skinny branch. In moments the pelicans would be dead and the golden eagle would be enjoying a rare meal. Hunting on this lake was becoming increasingly more difficult, and it would not be long until she would have to move further south, towards Lake of the Clouds, to find her next meal.

On Lake of the Clouds, Jake fished. It was not the best fishing waters. In fact he had never caught anything on the small lake yet. He had positioned himself in the exact middle of the water where he felt the safest. Wolves could not swim. At least, he didn't think so. Like his belief in a bear's inability to climb trees he was wrong again.

He had fashioned a sort of umbrella out of some balsam branches and the sheet from his bed. He was killing two birds with one stone. The first was to cover himself to keep from being roasted by the sun, and the second was to dry out his freshly lake-washed laundry. His mother would be proud.

The trapper sauntered out of the forest, apparently not worried about the wolf pack in the least. He was waving him in from shore. Jake pulled up his line, took note that his freshly dug earthworm was still alive and well, plucked it off the hook and dropped it in the tin can of wet mud that held three other squirmers, and slowly paddled in.

"What are ya fishin' here for?"

"What do you mean? Why not? Close to home."

"There ain't no fish in here. Too small for the big fish. Can't support 'em."

Jake frowned.

"Ever try Pike's Pond?"

Jake shook his head.

"Saddle up then. It'll blow your mind."

Pike's Pond was the weediest lake that Jake had ever seen. Its water was a greenish-brownish-bluish palette than seemed wavy despite the fact that there was no wind at all. "You wouldn't want to take a bath in here."

They had to step through chunky green weeds and ankle deep water to launch the canoe. The water was thick with northern pike; there were hundreds and hundreds of the fish, each one larger than the next. Their spotted backs were visible from looking down, impossibly long and thick. Ahead, two oily black eyes protruded the surface. As the canoe got closer, the big fish thrashed and bolted beneath the surface. "What the heck do all these fish eat?"

"Each other."

Jake shuddered. Every once in a while he could feel them scrape the bottom of the canoe with their backs. He reached for his tin of worms but the trapper waved him off. "Use this." He opened his hand to reveal a tattered piece of old rope. "Don't waste the good ones. These guys aren't picky."

Jake put his hook through the rope and tossed it into the water. It didn't even sink—just floated on the surface. It didn't have to sink, as the heaviest fish Jake had ever seen exploded from the water and took hook, line and rope four feet into the clear blue air, a flash of razor sharp teeth and blur of slimy black snout, before it crashed back into the lake with a thunderous slap. The fish tore the thin rod clean from Jake's hands and he was lucky not to have tried to hold onto it. His breath caught in his throat and he heard the old trapper gasping with laughter behind him as his fishing pole was pulled beneath the considerable ripples.

Not quite done his laughing fit the trapper himself got a hit, and his rod bent into a u-shaped pretzel. He kept it steady with his strong arms and darted his hand in the water like a grizzly after a salmon. Slime squeezed through his fingers. He gripped it by the gills where his hand seemed to disappear and strained to get it in the boat where he swiftly put a knife blade through its brain to prevent it from thrashing around and swamping them. They could have sat there all day and caught as many as they wanted, but the fact was that there wasn't room for even one more.

When they returned home, Jake watched the trapper expertly cut the pike into thick steaks.

"Do you have a name?" Jake asked, "I mean a real first name?" It had just occurred to Jake that neither had ever addressed each other by name. The old man referred to Jake as "boy" or "son" and that was when he was being cordial. Jake didn't have a hot clue as to what the trapper's name was.

"Sure I got a name. Everybody got a name."

The ensuing silence made Jake think that he was in for a dramatic unveiling. It soon became clear that the information was not forthcoming at all.

"Well?"

"Well what? Names are just labels, son. Call me whatever you like."

Jake sighed in resignation and then went into the cabin. The trapper did not let his guard down as easily as his grandfather had.

Jake's mind wandered back to the map of the Gem Lakes that the trapper had given him last year. If not for that dried-up piece of parchment he and Claire would never have made it through the tangled terrain of the lakes.

He had recently started making a map of his own on a starched piece of birchbark and had drawn in the cabin and the lake but also added any other interesting areas that he came upon. He picked up the pencil out of the can and drew in an outline of a lake and marked PIKE'S POND in big letters in the middle. So far he had the plane crash site, the Creek With No Name and several batches of trees that were in the area. It was therapeutic for Jake to learn and care about his surroundings. He wondered if fifty years from now his map would end up in a boy's hands like his grandfather's had ended up in his.

The golden eagle caught the current of a warm west wind and soared with through wispy whorls of low white cloud.

The freak ducks were below her, bobbing on the surface of a choppy lake, and diving for minnows. The eagle circled until the green-headed male dove under the waves. She plummeted straight down in a deadly nosedive.

The ducks were compact and powerful in their own right, and they certainly outnumbered the eagle, but the flock of ducks' organizational skills ended after the flying "V" formation.

The eagle made very short work of the seven birds. Feathers floated on the water. A metallic-green head bobbed in the water, no longer attached to its body.

An hour later, Jake and the trapper passed the scene on the way to fish for burbot to get some much-needed oil in their diet.

"Do you think the wolves did this?" Jake wondered incredulously.

"Impossible," replied the bushman but even he did not sound completely convinced. Whatever had killed the ducks, it was enough to cancel the day's fishing.

With the feathery massacre still fresh in his thoughts, Jake lugged a shirt-full of round rocks from the edge of the lake to fill in the holes around their outdoor fire pit. The pit was just a shallow dug out that was semi-surrounded with flat rocks but it held the sparks and deflected the heat and those were the only two criteria that mattered in its hasty construction.

The old man was making short work of a chunk of birch, each short, powerful swing of the hatchet split off a perfect splinter no thicker than a pencil.

"You should try this you know. I can't stick around just to be to be your personal wood splitter."

Jake ignored the comment but plucked the hatchet from the trapper's hand nonetheless. He lined up the log perfectly and his swing hit smack in the center of his target but it did not split the hard wood. Not even close.

His skin reddened and he swung much harder the second time. The edge of the blade glanced off the side of the birch and the follow through narrowly missed his shin-bone. The old man snatched the small axe back.

"The third time you'll eviscerate yourself for Criss' sake!"

Mid-way through the second cup of tree root tea Jake's brain was buzzing like a chainsaw with a broken kill switch. He quickly sat down again before he tumbled head first into the fire. The brew was a tasteless broth with a grassy aftertaste. It was a transparent green color and Jake had bits of dirt and who-knows-what lingering in the bottom of his cup. "How do you drink this stuff?" he sputtered and shivered at the same time. The temperature had dropped, and for the first time in some time they had actually started a fire outside to keep warm.

The Mad Trapper chuckled. "Natural caffeine ... it's a nice companion out here ... it will warm the cockles of your heart. Granted, boy, you have to use your imagination. You think I like the idea of sucking down tree sap? No sir." He thrust the cup above his head with a flourish. "Today this is the finest Columbian coffee on the market. Tomorrow, maybe a French Roast. We'll see. Cheers." He raised his metal cup again.

Jake went to click his mug but ended up sliding off the log and landing flat on his back. He had no idea what a cockle was, but if this tea would warm it up he was all for it.

Jake took a swig, sloshed it around his mouth and swallowed. Tasteless, dirty broth. "Hmmm, a triple-chocolate shake ...."

The trapper raised an eyebrow. "Well don't outright *lie* to yourself, boy."

Jake had surrounded the edges of the fire with about half a dozen fist-sized rocks. The trapper had taught him a trick to warm the core of his body by first warming rocks around the fire and then stuffing them in his shirt. It worked quite well because the rocks took as long to cool as they did to heat. He touched the one closest to his feet. It needed another ten minutes or so. He swatted at the bugs that were winding in and out of the fire's smoke.

The forest seemed to be a never-ending revolving door of bugs. The black flies did not bite at night but in the daytime would swarm in colossal numbers and menace your ankles and legs if you were in a canoe, or find your nostrils, ears, or hair if on land. They were drawn to darker clothes, which the old man favoured.

They'd appeared before the mosquitoes, as soon as the trees leafed out. Now, in late June, they'd passed the baton to the mosquitoes and no-see-ums, which were unbelievable, if not indescribable. "Swarms" did not give the situation justice. They somehow got into the cabin as if the door had been left open for hours. They hid in his hair, ears, under his clothes, leaving awful welts everywhere.

Then the fish flies had come.

One night they descended on the lake and covered every square inch of the front cabin wall. They smothered the rails and the deck. They blacked out the windows. They stayed exactly one day, did significant damage to the mosquito population and then died—every single one of them.

The stinking rot had to be swept off of every surface, and Jake had to shovel them off and bury them in the sand.

The worst however, were the horse flies, which the trapper referred to as "bulldogs." Jake had only seen the trapper show anger a handful of times. Each time had involved the bulldogs, which the old man had said could take half a litre of blood from a decent sized moose in one day. Jake himself was currently missing a few good-sized chunks of his neck from the giant insects.

He felt like his head was flying through the clouds. Natural caffeine was going to take some getting used to especially since he had never even drunk a full cup of regular coffee before. If he concentrated it tasted very vaguely like maple syrup and, well, tree root.

The old trapper's stomach seemed to be made out of cast iron. Some of the things that Jake had seen him eat had turned his own stomach in disgust.

The old man didn't even boil his drinking water, which as far as Jake remembered, was the cardinal rule of outdoor survival. If he was thirsty, he simply dipped his cup into the nearest lake, stream, or puddle and chugged it back. "Cleanest water in the world I'd wager," he'd say. "The whole bloomin' country had this water before they became dumps for lazy nogoodniks!"

In the silence that followed the trapper's scolding of society, Jake strained his ears. He heard a hissing.

Snake? "Do you hear that?" he asked. It had morphed from hissing to the sound of bacon sizzling. "What the heck is that?"

The trapper put down his cup. "Where'd you get those rocks?"

"The lake."

"The lake?"

The sizzling became deafening.

"Get down!" roared the old man.

Whether it was the dizzying effect of the tea, or the fact that Jake thought the trapper was giving him the gears, Jake did not get down even as he saw the trapper throw himself backwards off the log.

One of the rocks exploded with a resounding crack and a quarter sized chunk pelted Jake right between the eyes. He fell backwards off his own log.

"Stay down!"

Jake was too stunned to do anything else.

Another pop, then another: they were under missile attack from their own campfire. Bits of rocks and dust sprayed the two men.

Jake counted off three more explosions before he ventured to sit up. He touched the bridge of his nose where the rock had struck and came away with a palm full of blood.

"Is it broke?" the trapper asked, peering over the log.

"No, I don't think so," he gurgled blood and spat it into the offending fire pit. "What happened?"

"Those lake rocks have a lot of moisture in 'em. You heated it too fast, and made bombs out of 'em. You gotta use *dry* rocks."

"Huh uh. Lesson learned," he grunted and spit.

"One of a thousand ways you can kill yourself out here."

They checked the perimeter of the fire to make sure there were no other rock grenades and re-established their seats.

"Your ineptitude has inspired me."

"How so?"

"We have to destroy their den," the trapper mentioned casually as Jake waited for his face to clot.

"Whose den?"

"The wolves. They've gone plumb crazy. I thought Rusty was a once in a lifetime fluke—wrong place, wrong time— but my traps have been wiped clean twice now. Not even a bone left behind. At this rate they'll be donning yellow rainsuits and fishin' poles and pulling the fish right from the water. With no food there's no home for you here."

"You didn't tell me about the traps."

"You didn't notice we've been eating fish stew for a week straight?"

"Trust me I noticed that. I just thought you were losing your knack."

"Hah! I knew it! You thought the old man had a foot in the grave!"

Jake quickly moved to shift the subject before the bushman went on another rant. "How does destroying their den help us?"

The trapper looked up, unblinkingly. "They'll be *in* it at the time."

"Oh. I may regret this question but, well, how are we going to find it?"

"You forget I'm a trapper. B'sides, I have a good guess. I just got to check on it."

"Well what to you plan on doing if we find them?"

"By my reckoning there's only one way to do it up right."

Jake was quite sure that he did not want to know the trapper's solution. "How?"

"Well, how do you get rid of a beaver dam that's floodin'? How do you get rid of rock to set a rail down? How do you make a big ol' oak stump disappear?"

"I don't know."

"Dynamite. Nature's problem solver." His eyes glimmered like those of a man who enjoyed blowing things up. Jake developed an instant case of butterflies.

"There's only the small matter of actually findin' some dynamite."

Jake bolted upright and snapped his fingers. "There's dynamite in those stone igloos by the mine! We saw some in there last year."

The Mad Trapper arched an unruly eyebrow. "Blow 'em sky high we could. I wonder if it's got any bang left. I reckon there's only one way to find out."

Jake was not on board the trapper's wolf extermination plan. "Why don't we just let them be? They'll leave us alone—they'll die pretty soon won't they?" Jake still could not fully comprehend that the friendly pack had turned on his grandfather. The only explanation was that they were sick and if they were that diseased then how much longer could they last?

"Son, I'm not sure if you noticed but those wolves are devouring the forest. If we're the last two hinds of beef in the butcher shop, you can bet where the butcher will be. And what do you think they'll do when they're done with us? They'll go to the next food source a few miles south of here."

"Where?"

Apparently he was going to have to spell it out for the boy, "Lampshine Lake. You may have heard of it."

Terrible images blossomed in Jake's brain: the wolves flooding the sand paths and methodically pulling people out of their gardens, their woodpiles, their sheds and cabins; tearing them to pieces with no regard whether they were men, women, children or dogs. They were meat.

"Boy," the trapper said simply, "it's them or us."

"Okay. Where do we start?"

Susan sat on the dock wrapped in a blanket holding an empty wine glass and staring up at the pulsating stars. The night was breathing. A slight breeze blew through her hair and she brushed some stray strands from her eyes.

The winter had been much easier than this. She had immersed herself in activities she had never before considered. She joined a curling league every Wednesday even though she hadn't thrown a rock since high school. She took up oil painting with less than optimistic results and read more books than she had in three whole years before.

When it was finally time to come down to the lake for the summer, she subconsciously clamped up the moment she shut her door and Bob had turned the key to start the engine. As the distanced themselves from the city limits, they passed empty farmer's fields, some with blackened husks of last season's cornfields, which reminded her of death. The white lines on the highway seemed to be links of a chain that were pulling her closer to a nightmare, each bar that passed beneath the car one more foot closer.

She alternately imagined Jake traipsing around the lake having a grand old time whittling bow and arrows from the trees trunks, bringing down animals at will to feast on, and then having that image replaced by one of him being pulled apart by wolverines, or having to eat his own fingernails to avoid starving to death.

She had tuned the radio to the country station, which she ordinarily hated. But, it fit her mood better and dulled the edge of uncomfortable silence that had filtered into the car.

Still, the moment their car had pulled off the main highway onto that dirt road, her heart sank into her stomach. By the time they had arrived at the parking lot her knuckles were white, gripping the sides of her seat. She had noticed that Bob had a matching pair: a death grip on the steering wheel.

The last time she had come to Lampshine Lake she had left without her son. Now, several months after closing the car door in the parking lot she could not help but peer through the door to her future. With each passing day of staring optimistically into the forest behind the cabin she had managed to convince herself that whatever may roam the Gem Lakes couldn't be nearly as bad as the thoughts that roamed her head each and every hour. She sighed and pursed a small nervous smile on her lips. A decision had been made.

Part Two

THE CROW WAS FLYING IN A RAGGED LINE through a low cloud cover keeping a keen eye on the movements of the wolf pack below. They were on the move, trotting at a good pace through the forest. The pack followed the white leader who weaved quickly through the trees, and easily leapt over low lying brush and the occasional rock. The bird could not see anything that the wolves had been chasing, which meant that they were merely trying to get somewhere. If they stayed the present course and kept up their speed then they would easily be at the Lake of the Clouds by nightfall. The crow soared into the thinner atmosphere and picked up his pace. He would beat the wolves by an hour if he caught a favourable air current.

When he awoke his skin felt oily from the campfire smoke. His hair smelled the part as well. When he opened the door on his way to wash in the lake he was startled to find a large crow standing on the front step of his porch. Jake made a cautious move forward expecting the bird to fly off and when it held its ground Jake stopped. The wildlife out here still made him nervous and he had seen re-runs of an old bird movie where they started attacking people. He took a step back. The crow hopped up onto the rail.

Jake backed into the cabin and closed the door.

When he turned to look out the window the bird was there perched on the sill. It spread its wings and cawed loudly. Jake fell back.

The pack of wolves was skulking around on the opposite side of the Lake of the Clouds waiting for the boy to come out of the cabin. When darkness fell, the boy, wisely, did not often stray outside.

The night sky was clear and overflowing with stars. The moon was full and white and causing the wolves to tremble in excitement. One of the smaller animals could contain itself no longer and let out a blood curdling howl. The albino leader immediately pounced on its back, driving the offending muzzle into the grass harshly. It was not the time for noise.

Jake had heard the short-lived howl over an hour ago but nothing but suspicious silence since. He held a fire poker in a death grip and had propped a chair against the door with no lock. He did, however, have a major problem. The strange-acting crow had hung around the cabin for hours and Jake had not ventured out for fear of being pecked and now he needed to use the biffy in a bad way. A terrible twisting in his guts was imploring him to move.

The biffy was fifty feet behind the cabin.

He had sworn that the wolf must be close because he was pretty sure the howl had rattled the brittle glass of the window in its frame. The longer he thought about it, the closer the wolf had seemed. But when it got right down to it, when a guy had to go, a guy had to go!

Finally, he moved the chair and opened the door a crack. He peeked outside, half expecting the entire pack to be on the porch with tongues hanging out. There was nothing.

He took the poker with him and the heft of it gave him comfort. It wasn't one of those cheap campfire pokers either but forged steel that had three solid prongs on the end in a fleur-de-lis design that made for a very effective poker and a very nasty weapon.

He tried to walk a few normal paced steps but it quickly morphed into a trot, and then a full-blown sprint. He got to the biffy in record time and slammed the door behind him. The moonlight filtered through the moose-antlered shaped hole in the door and lit the interior of the outhouse.

By the funky smell drifting from the wood, the biffy itself only had a few more seasons left in it before a new hole would have to be dug. He did what he had to do and grabbed the poker. He opened the door and stepped back onto the path.

The wolves had been watching as the door opened, and the boy had come out and ran behind the cabin. Whines and growls emitted from the rest of the pack except the one that had already been disciplined who now slinked behind the rest. They moved forward, single file, following a deer path along the waters edge and slinked into the dark treed area behind the cabin.

Jake, feeling much better now, couldn't help noticing how still the night was. He did not know exactly what it was that made him turn around — perhaps it was *too* quiet and he was able to just slightly notice the padded paw stalk on the soft ground behind him — but whatever it was, he stopped in his tracks.

Its body passed through the moonlight and the shadowy darkness. A shard of light caught a wide gleaming eye. If there had been no moon he would not have even been able to see the wolf.

Memories of the joaquin charging at him after a standoff flashed through Jake's mind, but the wolf didn't give him a chance to think. Not thinking might have saved his life.

The animal charged — Jake could not tell if there were others around. In three bounds the white wolf leapt and swatted, as Jake instinctively brought the poker down as hard as he could.

Both the wolf and boy made contact as Jake's cheek spilled warm blood down his face and the poker smashed a dent in his attacker's skull.

The rest of the pack was indeed around and they flowed out of the forest invisibly and inexplicably went after their dazed leader instead of Jake. Never one to hang around and ask questions of a bloodthirsty wolf pack, Jake picked himself up and ran for his life.

The leader however, was down but definitely not out. He roared in frustration and fury, and fought back the pack. By the time they realized that their leader was not nearly ready to be dethroned Jake had scrambled back to the safety of the cabin.

This time he pushed the chair, the table, *and* the bed against the door. He had a terrible headache and was worried that he may have a concussion. Moonlight shone through the room across the floorboards. The cabin darkened occasionally as the gigantic wolves moved in front of the window, blocking the light of the moon. He heard bumps on the glass and the frame rattle. The boards on the porch creaked.

He stared at the poker, which was now bent at a forty-five degree angle. He did not sleep for hours, worried, knowing that the wolves could come through the window at any time if they wanted to. He only drifted off to sleep when his eyes became so heavy he couldn't physically avoid it. If willow witches were real, he hoped one would come out of the dark woods and save him from the freakish terror outside right about now.

The next morning Jake awoke earlier than usual. He had slept fitfully and sporadically while keeping close watch out the window. The wolves had stayed outside the cabin throughout the night. The biggest one looked like it had resurfaced from the dead; white as moonlight, with a tongue it couldn't keep in its mouth.

Now, as he rose from the still made bed, the crooked steel poker resting on his chest, he saw that the sun was up. He poked his head above the windowsill and scanned the porch and lakefront for the wolves.

He removed the furniture from the path of the door and tiredly opened it to find the wolves gone, replaced with a family of five grouse enjoying the sunny morning six steps away from the porch. Despite still being weary, he killed four of them in short order. Such was life in the forest that you could hunt for days without seeing your quarry and then the next have them stroll by your front door.

In order to avoid any chance of running into the wolves, Jake skewered the meat with the bent poker and cooked it in the steel fireplace two at a time like giant marshmallows. He ate the wild chicken inside at the table.

The good-sized drumsticks reminded him of eating fried chicken back home, and the ridiculous amount of meat he would leave on the drumstick, only because it was dark meat. Back then he'd liked the white meat exclusively.

Now, on days when he might get one meal, he would suck the marrow from the bones.

He methodically stripped every shred of meat off and then stuck the wing bone in his mouth to savour every morsel of flavour. He picked his teeth clean with his tongue. By the time he'd finished one bird there was nothing left but a pile of bones.

He thought about saving two of them for later, but instead ate three right away, and saved one for the trapper who appreciated it very much when he returned later that morning.

The trapper walked slowly around the perimeter of the cabin wondering how it was possible that he hadn't heard the wolves from the other side of the lake. Enormous paw prints were all around the building. "Jesus, they must weigh over three hundred pounds! Look how deep these tracks are...."

As the summer rolled along, June melted into July. A heat wave gripped the Interlake region, which in the last few days of July especially was proving to be both unbearable and inescapable. Bob had completely given up on fishing as the pickerel had disappeared into cooler water. Susan had been avoiding the dead air around the dock by staying in the relative coolness of the cabin.

A little deeper in the forest, at Lake of the Clouds, Jake had finally sacrificed one of his few t-shirts and fashioned it into a bandana to cover his neck and shoulders. He pulled his ball cap over that to successfully shadow his face. He sat around listlessly, only moving to wade into the lake up to his neck. The water seemed only a few degrees cooler but even that was a big difference.

Not far away, certainly not as far as Jake would have liked, the beer bottles floated in stagnant stillness as the semi-drought had affected every creek and river in the Gem Lakes Range. With no wind and little current the remaining bottles floated aimlessly, some even drifting back towards the starting line.

On the bright side of things, the heat seemed to have a crippling effect on the mosquito population as well. They were baking alive with no standing water around to support their never-ending larvae.

As he left the lake the oppressive heat pressed down on Jake and threatened to flatten him against the earth. He studied the treetops intently for even the slightest hint of wind. Not one leaf stirred. He took in lungfuls of syrupy air with each breath. The moisture he took in was in turn flushed from his system in jumbo beads of sweat along his skin.

Sleeping was difficult, as Jake could not stand to lie in the bed even when it was stripped of sheets. Instead, the relative coolness of the floor was glorious.

The wolves had taken to sleeping in whatever shadows they could find during the day, and hunting only at night. Jake never left the cabin at night anymore.

The golden eagle was enjoying the hot weather very much, as did most of the big predators and scavengers because, quite simply, things tended to die in the heat.

The first one to follow the smell of decomposing flesh received an easy meal. Not only that, but the more difficult prey would move into vulnerable positions, seeking to cool down in swamps or streams, which severely limited their mobility. It was after feasting on such an opportunistic meal of a heat-exhausted martin that the eagle discovered beer bottle number nine. The great bird grasped the shiny object in her talons and brought it back to her nest, which needed some shoring up in the structural department. It seemed like fine building material. Smooth and curved, it would serve as a splendid support for a weakening wall.

The earth has one tried and true way to cool itself after a heat wave. Jake had been expecting it for days, but was no less startled to walk out onto his porch one late afternoon only to see a sky that looked like a three-day old bruise, sickly yellow and black.

Whenever he spotted a dark cloud push its way into the heart of the sky his ribcage tightened like the skin over a drum. There was a well-known Canadian expression that said if you don't like the weather just wait for five minutes and it'll change. In the Gem Lakes you were content with whatever weather was happening at the time, because whatever blew in behind it could very well knock you on your tailbone.

Cold air drifted low across the lake and swept across his face like the sky was firing a shot across the bow in warning. Soon the wind followed, hard and high, stirring up white caps on the small lake, bending the balsam trees enough to get Jake's pulse racing. There were lumbering black clouds converging from three different directions, moving quicker than Jake could ever remember seeing. The strange silence unnerved him. A static electricity surged through the air, and made Jake's hair stand on end.

And then everything stopped. The sound was sucked out of the air as if the storm had a vacuum attached to it.

He watched from the porch until the first drop of rain pelted him on the lip and then went inside to wait it out.

Back at Lampshine the storm had come up quickly while both Lucknows had been well into their mid-afternoon naps. Bob drifted in and out of sleep while the a.m. radio crackled static and news from the other room. He barely made out something about a cottage country storm warning and then snapped fully awake with the first clap of thunder. He lay listening to the pounding rain on the shingles and then leapt out of bed as he realized that the boat had not been turned around. He scrambled off the couch that was about two feet too short for him anyway and looked outside through the front windows.

Storm clouds heaved and rolled across the sky over the cabin, blackening as they steamed towards the Gem Lakes.

He could barely see the dock through the sheets of rain but he did manage to confirm his fears as the waves were rolling effortlessly over the transom that he couldn't even see and the boat was already sitting on the bottom of the lake, completely swamped. The top of the outboard motor was barely visible. Old Reliable was drowning.

"Susan! Get up! Grab the rainsuits!"

A funnel cloud spun out of the low clouds like gigantic drill bit. Jake knew that it was not called a tornado unless it actually made landfall but it made the rotating black clouds no less terrifying.

The panes of glass rattled in their frames, and Jake strained to hear the low whine of what sounded like a locomotive. By the trees and dirt and water kicking up off the ground about a mile away, Jake ruled out the possibility of a train. Tornado.

Jake gasped as the violent column of wind touched down, lifted and set down again, as if it were merrily skipping along the countryside.

Jake finally found his feet after the funnel cloud twisted down from the clouds beyond the treeline. He witnessed a tree uproot near the lake and fall heavily into the water. Bark exploded off nearby tree trunks, leaving them completely stripped.

He dove under the sturdy metal frame of the bed, which might shield him from the roof if it caved in, but would protect him from little else. A school project had told him that most tornado damage to buildings happened when the wind picked up outside objects and fired them like missiles at or through the walls. He imagined a forest worth of trees landing on top of him.

The wind ripped across the small lake, screaming as it pounded the windows in their frames. He could hear pieces of the roof tear away. Sure enough, a tree crashed down with a resounding bang—not penetrating the shingles, but poking a hole through the entire top frame of the side window. Jake whimpered as rain swept in sideways. He prayed out loud, trying to out-shout the wind, that no more trees would come down.

Although it was one of the furthest things from his mind, deep in the forest Jake's beer bottles were on the move again. They were moving at breakneck speed now, so much so that bottle number ten and eleven smashed together in a torrent of white waves.

The lightning was constant and when one storm moved away, another slid on in, leaving Jake to cover his head for over six terrible hours.

Through it all he could hear the faint lunatic howls of wolves.

Jake awoke with an awful crick in his neck—at one point during the night he had passed out under the bed and had pulled his half soaked blanket from the top of the bed for comfort. When he finally crawled out from underneath, hours later, he saw the pain in his neck was the least of his problems.

A red sky dawn washed the bent white birches pink. The air was dead, as dead as you could ever see it. The forest was quiet. The smell of pine and rain was suspended in the mist like smoke from a farmer's stubble burn. Somewhere very far off a train whistled through the granite hills.

The damage was obvious and alarming. Trees were cracked; pushed over like dominoes, uprooted and moved without effort. Some had bark that had been sheared right off the trunks.

A dead fish was impaled against a drying hook on the front cabin wall, which was a testament to the length of the twister's path as there were no fish in the Lake of the Clouds.

The food cache that had been in the tree still was but that particular tree was now shattered on the rocky ground with the cache itself a pile of splinters within the tangled mass of snapped branches.

As he surveyed the damage he noticed that the only trees that weren't blown over or leaning were the three poplars that loomed over the cabin as if in defiance of his earlier doubt.

With his choices limited to feeling sorry for himself or getting busy rebuilding, he chose the latter. He choked down a lump in his throat.

He turned his attention to the first priority—the broken window on the east wall—and started by cutting the mid-sized tree in half with the band saw from the woodpile, which had completely blown apart and scattered. He was lucky that the roof had held back the thick trunk with only one large branch doing most of the damage. He could not replace the glass so he pulled out some ancient two-by-fours and tried to nail them over the open space before all the bugs in the forest had made themselves at home.

As Jake carefully removed the shards of glass that remained in the frame he noticed that there was a considerable space between the header and the log above it. It looked like an intentional space.

He frowned and reached his hand in, weary of spiders or mice, and pulled out a shotgun shell. Jake rolled the shell around his fingers. It had a faded green paper casing and the brass end had a few mottled black spots that looked like mould.

Reaching into the hidden hole again, he found five more shells—half a dozen in total. His grandfather must have hidden the shells there years ago. Maybe they didn't work anymore but they seemed to look okay. Maybe his grandfather had forgotten where he had put them. He seemed to remember him saying that he had run out and been unable to get more.

Jake stared at the shells for some time as a parcel of cold air suddenly came through the door as he realized he was holding the very items that may have saved his grandfather's life. If only he had known where they were.

Jake's had not been the only home disturbed by the brutal storm. The golden eagle's nest had been torn to shreds and scattered over the water. Indeed, she had nearly been ripped apart by the cyclonic winds as well.

She had found refuge in the crevice of a rock shelf, quickly dispatching the small family of mice that had been nesting there. Now, in the calm of the aftermath, it was time to rebuild.

The location of the new nest was not arbitrary or random but strategic and calculated. The main criterion was the proximity of a food source and the eagle had to fly a fair distance south before she came across any prospective real estate. As she circled a small lake from miles overhead, she noticed a cabin near the shore, and a boy outside surveying the storm damage.

The eagle had found her food source.

"Helluva storm last night. Unbelievable!"

"You're telling me—that poplar came down right on my barbeque. I'm lucky it didn't take the entire deck out!"

"Those clouds over past Timber Wolf were something else."

Lionel Clump was changing the sparkplugs in his chainsaw with the help of his friend and neighbour, Dick Mclinktok, when the conversation eventually turned towards the summers hottest gossip: just what the heck was going on over at the Lucknow cabin?

The lake community rumour mill had been churning out some dandy ones ever since the military had invaded the lake last year. Nobody had seen the Lucknow boy since.

The Gem Lakes were like the ultimate skeleton in the closet. Everybody knew they were there but absolutely nobody talked about them. They just sat there in the distance, lurking in a not-so-faraway forest.

"Pass me the wrench, would you, Dick?"

"Sure thing. Hey did you hear the latest scuttlebutt on the Lucknow kid?"

Lionel wiped his sweaty forehead with a greasy hand and left a black streak on his hairline. "That he was born with gills and that they put him back in Timber Wolf so he could live in an underwater city?"

"Like Atlanta?"

"Atlantis?"

"Oh yeah, right. No, no not that one. The one where he fell down an old flooded mine shaft and that he's surviving on rainwater and eating bats. That he's eaten so many bats that he's got infrared vision now. They can't get him out so he's just … living there."

"That's bull, Dick. Who told you that garbage?"

"It's what I heard," he said, somewhat defensively.

"Well, I heard that the kid had a tumour in his head— that they couldn't operate so he just went for a walk one day and died out there." He nodded towards the direction of the Gem Lakes. "Never found the body."

"Maybe that's because he's at the bottom of a mine shaft, eatin' bats."

"Maybe." He tightened the last of the new plugs and replaced the engine cover. "Good as gold."

"Say, did you hear those wolves the other night?"

Lionel put down the wrench, a wave of concern washed over his face. "Yeah, sounds like they got a hold of something big. We were sitting on the dock. Went inside when they started up. Sounded close," he shivered.

"Yeah. It was pretty creepy." Dick didn't want to admit that he had thought the howling was so creepy that he had locked the doors to the cabin for the first time in twenty-five years.

Jake awoke on the morning he was never supposed to see and mumbled to himself, "Happy birthday …."

He wasn't one hundred percent sure that it was his birthday. It could have been yesterday or two days down the road.

Somewhere along the line he had lost track of a Monday or a Tuesday, and as the days blended seamlessly together into long stretches of weeks and months Jake couldn't ever be sure exactly what day it was. He had stopped trying to keep track. He'd simply decided that today would be the day he celebrated. It was close enough.

The trapper had gotten wind of his birthday as well, as Jake had been droning "Happy Birthday to me" under his breath all morning. He was not about to let the day pass without incident. In fact, the incident would be monumental.

"Fifteen, eh? You're a man now."

"I thought that was eighteen," Jake replied.

"Not out here, my friend. If you're old enough to bring back dinner you make the grade."

Jake was somewhat confused since he had become a mildly successful fisherman and grouse hunter over the summer. The old man could see the wheels spinning in Jake's head. "I don't mean table scraps. I mean real meat, boy. Something you can sink your teeth into. I mean it's time you joined me on a real hunting trip."

Jake sat straight up in attention. He had often asked to go, but had always been told to stay on Lake of the Clouds and "hold the fort" instead.

"What? Really? What are we hunting? When are we going?"

He held up a hand to slow the youngster down. "We are leaving tomorrow morning—before sunrise. There's a bull moose hiding out in the ravine a few miles south."

"A moose? Isn't that a little big for my first hunt?"

"Might as well start at the top, boy. Anyway, the circumstances are in our favour. The ravine gives us better odds than open forest."

"I thought you said the moose went to the ridge to get away from the bugs."

"Ah, you *are* paying attention to me after all. It's true, but now there are bigger thorns on the vine than insects. A swarm of wolves is always more irritating than a swarm of skeeters. You can write that down."

"How are we going to kill it?"

"We are going to need to work together. It's going to be very dangerous. I wouldn't ask you to do it if I didn't think you were able."

"How?"

"Spears. Very long spears."

"Spears," Jake repeated.

The trapper picked up a stick and started etching out the ambush in the sand like drawing up plays for a beach football game. "The ravine has granite walls on either side. It's a creek in the spring, mostly dry now except for the soft middle, which will be a mucky mess. We'll have to come down either side of the rock and make it to the edge of this long grass that's on either side." He pointed to two places on his sketch on either side of the muddy middle.

Beside the small map was another sketch of a moose. "We'll have two chances to hit the heart. Front shoulder between the ribs. The most important thing is to push that spear with absolutely everything you've got. I don't want this old boy to suffer. If you hesitate, you won't get through the hide and all your tombstone will say is that you're the damn fool that walked up and whacked a moose in the ribs with a stick. "For God's sake be careful. If he catches you with that rack you'll be looking for a new head."

The reason the trapper didn't give Jake more notice of the hunt was two-fold. One, he had chanced upon the moose just a day ago and was not sure how much longer the old boy would be able to evade the savage wolves. Two, he didn't want Jake to over think the situation or get nervous.

They had pulled the two giant spears from under the cabin. Jake had never known they were there. The old man passed one to him. "This was your grandfather's. He was an expert with it even with one hand."

The spear was basically a small thin tree that was straight as an arrow and carefully sharpened to an incredibly fine point. It was heavy. The trapper watched Jake fumbling with it awkwardly. "Thankfully, you don't have to throw it."

Jake looked relieved and then realized what the alternative was. "You mean we're going to—"

"If you want to pull the plug at anytime just let out a yelp. But there is no turning back once we break the bush. You understand? Here, grip it like this."

The sun's first light took its time warming the cool morning. The moose hunters had made it to the ravine while it was still dark so they sat on the top of the rocky ravine and waited until they could see. Jake passed on the swig of tree root tea from the canteen.

The pair used hand signals to the point of the bog and then spotted the great animal in the middle munching mindlessly on the tubers and roots of the lush greens. The plan was to climb down opposite sides of the ravine from each other and make absolutely no noise. Above all, they wanted to avoid sending the gigantic beast straight at the other. The old man motioned that he was going to cross the ravine further down the rock. Jake nodded, and waited to make his own descent. His heart was thumping.

As he made his way down the dry granite, Jake was very careful not to break the pointed tip off the spear. Despite the fact that it was likely sharp enough to sew buttons on a silk shirt, he wasn't sure it was sharp *enough*. He crouched down in the long grass and looked for the trapper. Of course, he was already there.

The moose was ridiculously large, maybe even bigger than the one that had chased him and Claire through the bear caves last summer. Its long skinny legs supported the nearly eighteen hundred pound behemoth with little trouble. Its hide was covered in black flies.

The animal was a formidable sight and an unnerving prey. Jake fought back the dry heaves. Living this deep in the bush Jake had seen more than his fair share of monstrous moose. Now, looking up to the underside of its belly, he froze. It was clear that Mother Nature had designed this particular animal to be very hard to kill.

They were supposed to wait until the moose reached for food or water and as he dipped his snout into the puddle in front of him the grass parted on the opposite side.

Jake sprang from the grass at the same time as the trapper, who ran very quickly for an old man. The bull's head bolted straight up, like it had been attached to heavy-gauged puppet strings, and glared in Jake's direction first. He heard the man coming from the other side and instinctively shoulder checked him as well. The moose bucked forward making a charge straight ahead but was hit by both assailants at once, taking its considerable breath away.

The moose bellowed. The old man cursed. Both spears had pierced the flesh but missed their mark.

With his spear sunk an impressive depth into the obviously undead moose, Jake quickly realized that they hadn't actually accounted for this particular problem. He gripped the spear with both hands and pulled back but couldn't budge it. The moose's head swung towards him. Hot mucus from its flaring nostrils sprayed his face. Air bubbles popped as the animal's legs lifted out of the mud.

Its black eyes pierced Jake's and the moose bucked again, this time sending Jake and the spear flying all the way back into the grass where he landed on his back with a thud. His eyes rolled into the back of his head.

When the animal turned to do the same to the old man he was waiting for it with his spear cocked behind his back. "Well played, old boy," and he sunk the weapon between the two ribs he had barely missed the first time.

Jake was up on his elbows with the wind knocked out of him. "How many times do you get picked up off the ground in a year?"

"That was intense."

"That was the easy part."

While it was a feat in itself to bring the moose down without major personal injury there was no possible way that the two of them were going to be able to move the carcass from the ravine. They needed to work fast. The wolves would be attracted to the blood.

Gutting the moose was the most disgusting, horrible smelling, messiest, bloodiest, grossest fly-infested thing Jake had ever participated in. He vomited three times during the process. Afterward, he'd washed his hands for a solid hour, and still had intestines under his fingernails.

In the end they packed out nearly four hundred pounds of meat in two trips. The rest wouldn't last through night. They loathed wasting it but felt that they had pressed their luck with the wolves and still had much to do.

Jake was thoroughly exhausted when they returned to the cabin. Their work, however, was not quite done, as they had to cure the meat by hanging it in smoke until it formed a protective crust. The flies were all over them during every second. Before the meat was hung, the trapper cut off two generous hunks and kept them aside.

Finally they were able to wash up and Jake changed into clothes that weren't saturated in moose guts. He figured he would have to burn the clothes in the next fire.

The day had started in the dark and now Jake noticed that the daylight was already fading. It had been a very long day.

It was in fact Jake's birthday and Bob and Susan had been avoiding each other since they had gotten out of bed that morning. Even the cabin seemed to be in a sombre mood; chilly on the inside despite the warmth of the day outside.

Bob had gone fishing in Jake's favourite spots using one of his son's favourite Red Devils, while Susan had cooked

Jake's favourite breakfast, and ate it alone at the kitchen table. If there was one harsh reality that set in just a little deeper every single day, it was that the world did not seem to care in the least about the Lucknow state of affairs. The sun continued to rise and set every day. Minutes ticked away into hours. Time rolled on.

The moose steaks sizzled in their own juices, and the smell made Jake's insides clench with anticipation. When the outsides had seared almost black, the old man removed them, and passed Jake a tin plate that was overflowing with moose meat.

"You can't get a birthday dinner like this back in the city can you?"

Jake shook his head. "It's a little more work than going to the grocery store or a restaurant."

"Yes, but the satisfaction of a good day's work makes it taste better."

The trapper was right. Jake cut into the hot meat and slid a piece off his knife and into his mouth. The flavour was unbelievable and so juicy it made Jake want to cry.

"I reckon I know where they're at."

"Who?" Jake asked. He answered his own question, "The wolves."

"On my side of the ravine this morning—a couple of sets of tracks. The pack had been watching that moose too. They've been sending a loner over to check it. Waiting for it to move. The tracks left heading north—to their den."

"Where?" Jake looked over his shoulder.

"Up there," he nodded to the west and Jake followed his gaze above the treeline to a high ridge in the shadowy distance.

"How do you know?"

"You find a lot of moose up there this time of year. It's windy. They like it cause its relief from the bugs. The wolves follow their food and besides that they like to be higher than everything else—to keep an eye on everything. They'll be easy to track, anyway. If all else fails we'll just follow the trail of blood and guts."

"We're going to need that dynamite. Tomorrow." And with that, the trapper got up to wash his hands—and hopefully his face, as he had moose juice smeared all over it.

Jake got up, rinsed his plate in the lake and headed towards the cabin.

Living in a forest wasn't all hardship and loneliness. It wasn't as though he'd been banished to a labyrinth of underground caves, or shot out into outer space or something.

Remarkable things happened everyday if you were just willing to step out the door and look for them. Jake didn't have to step too far off the beaten path—or the last step of his porch—to see one of the most extraordinary things he had ever witnessed.

Hundreds of thousands of dragonflies were hovering and darting around the shore of the lake, like a fleet of miniature helicopters. It was a feeding frenzy.

The dragonflies were no fools and knew when and where the biggest mosquitoes congregated. When the sun started to set and the wind died down, it was usually the time Jake retreated to the cabin, as the bush buzzed alive with bugs. On this evening, however, he was out in shirtsleeves, as the mosquitoes were too busy scrambling for their lives to be worried about Jake's exposed flesh. The dragonflies shimmered green, purple and gold against the pink sky, and to Jake it was a fine substitute for candles on a cake.

Following her children's path into the Gem Lakes was going to take all the courage and determination that Susan Lucknow had to muster. It was also going to take one simple thing that she did not have: a mode of transportation.

She thought that physically she could handle carrying a canoe by herself, as long as the portages were short enough, but the fact of the matter was that the Lucknow's only canoe was currently seven hundred feet below the surface of Ruby Lake. She could not borrow a canoe from a neighbour without the threat of Bob getting wind of it. That left her only one option. As her husband went off to the front yard with the weed-whacker, she went around the back and peered beneath the underbelly of the cabin. The faded blue kayak was still there lying upside down on two two-by-fours in the sand. It had been there, untouched, for ten years. Susan had been an avid kayaker in her day but it was one of those things that she had given up when time became scarce with kids and work, and had never had a chance to get back into it.

She dragged it out from the bottom and into the open. She brushed away the dusty cobwebs and was relieved to find the double-ended paddle still tucked away inside. The kayak was much lighter than the canoe would have been but had a major disadvantage in the cargo space category. There was a web of nylon mesh at the back that could handle a large backpack worth of stuff but not much else.

As she picked the kayak up over her head her muscles burned, and her shoulders creaked at the unfamiliar weight, but it was nothing she couldn't handle. She walked the boat up the rock, behind the woodpile, and stooped underneath the clothesline to pass under it. The path to Timber Wolf Lake ran behind the pile so she tucked the kayak between some trees and returned to the cabin. She smoothed out the mark in the sand where she had dragged the boat out and went back inside.

A group of lazy turkey vultures had taken to following the wolf pack and the carnage that inevitably came with them. The trouble was that the wolves weren't leaving much in the way of scraps. Bones, tendons and hooves were devoured with the same ferocity as the meat and organs. One of the birds had stooped to eating the stale flavoured birchbark paper out of a shattered beer bottle number thirteen, as well as a few chunks of the broken glass, before it realized that it wasn't the best for digestion, even by its low standards.

When one of the large scavengers bravely or stupidly wandered to close to one of the feasting beasts, its head was swiftly torn off and his still moving body quickly eviscerated into a pile of black feathers. The vultures didn't follow as close from then on in.

Bob stirred only slightly as his wife carefully left the warm comfort of their bed and walked slowly across the hardwood floor making sure not to step on the several boards that were well-known creakers.

He assumed that she was making a late-night trek out to the biffy, unusual for his wife because she was not a fan of foraying into the forest in the dark, but he reasoned, when you have to go, you have to go. By the time she had slipped out of the room and silently closed the door, he had fallen back asleep.

Susan made a quick stop in the kitchen and grabbed the plastic bag full of clothes that she had stuffed in the cabinet under the sink just after dinner. Bob, in his never-ending quest to avoid doing dishes, would never look underneath the sink, just in case he encountered a dirty plate or some liquid soap. She removed the rumpled clothes from the bag—sweat pants and a well-worn hooded sweatshirt—and pulled them over her celery green pyjamas. She put on the wool socks, and then made her way to the back door where she completed her ensemble with a pair of hiking boots and a black vest. Her final touch was a generous swipe of perfumed deodorant that the label claimed was a "Tropical Breeze" that would hopefully help cover up the sweat she was no doubt going to work up on her journey.

She stuffed the mosquito hat into her pocket, and stood facing the heavy door. She drew a very deep breath, pulled it open, and stepped into the darkness.

She stood on the back deck for what seemed like an eternity, waiting for her eyes to grow accustomed to the dark. She had made it this far twice before: once last summer, and once few weeks ago. Both times she had stood in the dark and scared herself out of her plan; the noises and the silence taking equal turns in terrifying her. She had been furious at herself the next day, unable to sleep, and restless, not able to screw on enough courage to go and find her son. This game had gone on quite long enough. A mother had to see for herself. She would decide about the future after that. She missed him terribly.

She stepped off the deck.

When Jake and the trapper came upon the sucker run at the mouth of the creek that flowed the short distance from Lake of the Clouds to Moonstone Lake, the water was so red Jake thought it was a bubbling brook of blood.

The sucker was quite possibly the ugliest freshwater fish known to man. Its human-like lips were on the bottom of the fish's face so it could, as the name suggests, suck up food from the lake bottom. When his father would catch them he would throw them back. Jake couldn't use the adjective that his father had used to describe the taste.

The trapper, however, licked his dry cracked lips. "Nothin' beats smoked sucker...."

Jake was sceptical. "How are we going to catch them with no rods ... no nets?"

"Don't need nothin' like that for sucker, boy, not when they're runnin' like this." With that, the Mad Trapper pulled up his pant-legs, and waded into the mouth of the creek up to his ankles, while the suckers flipped and flopped, hitting his scrawny, pale calves. He looked like somebody agonizing over which lobster to pick from a five-star restaurants tank. He hand shot out in the blink of an eye, and his calloused fingers came up with a fat fish, thrashing about madly to escape the trapper's iron grip.

"Aren't you gonna get one fer yourself? I ain't sharin' smoked sucker, boy."

Jake looked at the swarming suckers with dread. He thought he had put his fear of fish handling behind him but this was ridiculous. He did not, however, want to look like a fool in front of the trapper.

Jake rolled up his pant legs and waded into the creek himself. The slimy fish swam over his bare feet and rushed past his equally skinny and pasty legs. He was knocked off balance by the rushing red bodies, and fell on his back. The slippery suckers instantly swarmed him. He screamed, and in doing so swallowed a considerable mouthful of water. He was panicking.

The trapper reached in and pulled him out, reminding Jake of how his grandfather had pulled him out of the icy water in the spring. Jake choked and sputtered, his lungs aching for air. The old man pounded him on the back a few times with an open palm and Jake coughed up the water. He froze in terror again as he realized that there was something squirming underneath his soaking shirt. He started dancing wildly and pulling his shirt over his head, which only served to blind him, and over he went again, tripping over a fallen tree.

"And they call me Mad...," the trapper muttered under his breath.

Jake leapt to his feet and threw his shirt on the ground. Two suckers flipped and flopped right next to it. The trapper was impressed. "Well, looks like we've got 'nuff for breakfast."

A beam of warm morning sunlight found its way through the thin curtains in the Lucknow's bedroom and fell across the stubbled face of the man slumbering there. Bob sniffed and snorted as if he had been physically touched on the cheek, and then slowly opened one of his sleepy eyes. He noticed almost immediately that his wife had left the bed. But that was par for the course. She was not one for sleeping in. She was more than likely curled up in the rocking chair with a cup of coffee, and the latest drugstore mystery. Bob turned over, letting the sunbeam warm the back of his neck, and faded back to sleep.

Bob awoke again, this time to the pitter-patter of rain against the glass of the window. It was almost eleven o-clock now, and he stretched mightily, rubbing sleep-swollen eyes. He must have been tired.

He noticed a few little things almost absently. All the things by themselves would not have even registered in his brain, but together, they signified disturbing little pieces of an unsettling puzzle. The first cause for pause was that the coffee pot was not on the woodstove. Routine dictated that Susan would get up at her usual ungodly hour and put on a pot of brew. She would have her two cups and then leave the black liquid to slowly thicken to sludge as it waited for Bob to wake up. He would take his coffee black, and in whatever consistency and temperature he found it in, no matter what time he crawled out of bed.

The coffee pot was still perched on the hook above the stove... untouched.

He noticed Susan's hiking boots were missing as he tied on his own to go out to the biffy. That was strange since

Susan, ever since the Christmas that he had bought them for her, had treated them more like floor ornaments than walking shoes. She had, however, recently taken to jogging the front path to the road and running a few miles in the morning. Maybe today she had decided to walk.

The final piece should have slid into place somewhere in his under-caffeinated mind on his way back from the biffy when he noticed a black tail wagging from underneath the back corner of the cabin. "Buzz?" The neighbours three cabins down had an old black lab that patrolled the entire lake for breakfast scraps. Buzz had shown up like clockwork everyday of every summer for the last seven years. Buzz had never tried to get under the cabin.

The dogs face popped out from the cabin, expecting to see some leftover eggs and toast. When he saw that Bob was empty handed, he gave a disappointing yap and sprang out and down the path, onto the next buffet.

Bob crouched down from where Buzz had been hiding and furrowed his brow. The reason that Buzz had never been under the cabin before was that there had been no room for him. Now, there was a void. He scratched his whiskered chin. What the heck was missing?

It did not take long to realize that the dynamite from the two igloos that were still intact was not going to be useful in their quest to rid the Gem Lakes of the infected wolves.

"This is no good," the trapper frowned. "Too dry. We'll blow our hands off with this stuff. We need some dampness in it. Not so much that the powder's wet, but at least the wick. At the very least we need some oil to grease these wicks, or to find some blasting caps."

"Can't we just make a new fuse?"

The old man shook his head. "Dynamite is basically saw-dust soaked in nitroglycerin. As it ages, gravity pulls the ni-tro down and it seeps out," he pointed to the white crystals on the bottom of almost every stick. "That is some very sen-sitive stuff if you know what I mean."

Jake was disheartened. "Great. Now what?"

"Whoa there, boy, you give up too easily. We can get some good dynamite. From there." Jake followed the trap-per's gaze through the trees and into the black entrance of the Succa Sunna Mine.

"Oh no."

"Oh yes."

The Succa Sunna Mine entrance should have been boarded up long ago, its tunnels and the main shaft should have been flooded or filled in to prevent exactly what was hap-pening now. As the Mad Trapper and Jake peered inside it was obvious that this had never been attempted. The rem-nants of an old track weaved out of the mine and around the side that eventually led to a dilapidated sifter that once used water to separate gravel. The trapper munched on a blade of grass. "I've never been in here," he announced.

That was not what Jake wanted to hear at that particular moment. The *rants* still terrified him, even though they had seemed harmless — he could remember them running from the thunder last year, seeking cover in the mine. He was un-sure what to make of them. He had originally thought they were ghosts. His grandfather had rebutted that, explaining they were miners that were still alive and would only die if they stopped working.

He and Claire had first encountered them between Emerald and Sapphire Lakes when the rants had crept around their campsite last year. They had moved quickly back and forth between the trees and rambled through the dark until the two had been scared half to death.

Whatever they were, he didn't think that invading their precious mine was the proper way to introduce himself. Besides, if the rants only wandered the forest at night then it stood to reason that they were *in* the mine right now. Jake brought this theory up to the trapper.

He scoffed. "They're probably more skittish of you than you are of them."

The mine smelled, not unpleasantly, of old, wet wood. The timber reinforcements were gorged and swollen with condensation and most of the supporting joists were resting uselessly on the rocky floor. Jake could make out piles of rubble from old cave-ins but nothing that they couldn't get around.

"Now pay attention boy, there's tunnels that branch off all over the place. We don't want to get lost in here."

The trapper went first, shuffling along carefully so as not to plummet to his death down an open shaft. Despite the light from the entrance, the darkness ahead was overwhelming, to the point that Jake thought that whoever was in charge of making up names for colors would have to come up with something darker-sounding than "black." This darkness had a viscosity about it, something that Jake could feel in his lungs each time he inhaled.

"Drag your feet. If you lift 'em, you might put 'em down in a very deep hole."

There was long forgotten, broken-down equipment scattered about the narrowing tunnel. The chance of bumping into an old blade, or even stepping on a rusty nail was a danger that would become a very big problem once they were back out in the woods.

What they were searching for was the farthest point that the miners had gotten to before they had disappeared. Dynamite was not usually stored in the mine itself for obvious reasons. That was the point of the stone igloos. The trapper, however, figured there might be a few sticks around the next blast point.

As they scuffled along the ground beside the track, the trapper would stop occasionally, strike a match, and point out various tools that the miners had used back in the heyday of the place. A well used ore cart was pushed on it side, a wheelbarrow sat empty and ominous in the middle of the tunnel, old drive shafts were stacked in a neat, rusted pile. At one point, they found an open shaft only by noticing what they thought was an oil spill on the floor. The dark spot was actually a hole. The trapper picked up a loose rock and tossed it underhand into the shaft and they listened carefully for 30 full seconds without hearing it hit bottom. "Now that's deep — over a hundred fifty feet I reckon. The boys would have had to take this out a bucket at a time."

Jake could not imagine what the men must have gone through: working in the dark, carrying heavy loads of rock and ore, day in and day out.

Jake heard the trapper stop in front of him but couldn't see his hand stretched out in a "stop" signal until he ran into the open palm with his face. He stopped abruptly.

"Sshh!"

Jake strained to listen and heard the low whine almost immediately. It was coming from deep in the dark ahead of them. It was coming towards them. The rants!

"Get down and cover yer head!"

Jake, frozen like a deer in an eighteen-wheeler's headlights, was too slow and felt an enormous cold and clammy hand cover his face. Something screeched and something else pulled mightily on his hair and unable to see his attackers, Jake dropped into the fetal position and prepared to take a very thorough beating.

He soon realized that he was not being accosted by the creepy rants but by equally creepy bats: big, aggravated bats. They were invisible in the tunnel and Jake pulled the incensed flying rodent off his face, unable to discern its hissing over the maddening screaming and frenzied flying above him. He threw the assailant against the rocky wall and hit the deck in panic. The bats swooped down in gangs and banged both Jake and the old man's backs and heads with their oversized wings. There were hundreds and hundreds of them. One got under Jake's shirt, which was ten times worse than the sucker had been. It scratched or bit his skin before Jake pulled his shirt off, and began swinging it wildly above him.

He knocked down more than a few and took a couple more hits to the head and shoulders before they were returned to total silence.

The trapper got up slowly and dusted himself off. "Well then, I guess they was just passing through."

"Passing through? I think I got bit! They were trying to kill us!"

The trapper waved him off. "Bats are lazy. They go after the nearest thing they can handle. We was just in the way."

Susan's tears dried before the rainwater from her hair did. Her frustration with the bugs had morphed into a jaw-clenching anger. Her muscles tightened with determination. Hell hath no fury like a woman irritated. The bugs seemed to back off just a bit.

The wooden cart wheel stuck out of the ground like a garden ornament, looking like it might have been left there for aesthetics rather than abandoned like a piece of trash. A rusted metal plate was still valiantly holding it together.

She looked up through the trees and saw a clearing. She made her way through, and stood halfway behind a tree trying to figure out exactly what it was she was looking at. The mine, surely not active for decades, stood in front of her. It was a wall of rock, with a black hole for an entrance.

She was scared and a little bit excited. Both Claire and Bob had mentioned the mine while they had been trying to convince her of the dangers of searching for Jake. Susan did not believe for a second the ghost stories they had spun about this place and the men who used to mine here.

In fact, the story was so dubious that Susan now wondered if they had been trying to scare her away from this place for a reason. Maybe this is where Jake was. It certainly looked like a place that her adventurous son would be interested in.

She crept closer to the entrance. She put one hand on the edge and peered inside. The darkness was immediate and impenetrable. She took another look behind her because she had a very bad feeling that something was watching her. She saw nothing. The forest was still. She called into the mine for her son.

"Oh my God ... did you hear that?"

The trapper stopped and slowly nodded. "I did hear that."

There were voices coming from the entrance. The rants were back and Jake and the old man were caught inside. The noises were unintelligible, bouncing off the rock and echoing from all around. They grew louder and louder.

Jake felt a hand on his arm. It was the trapper, pulling him to the side.

"In here, quickly!"

They seemed to walk through the rock and right into a hidden alcove. They waited ten full minutes and did not hear another sound. "Do you think they're waiting out there?"

"I doubt it."

Jake kicked something solid. "Ouch, what was that?"

The trapper knelt and felt around until he touched a wooden box. Upon further inspection they found half a dozen more. "This could be what we're looking for."

"Do you want me to light another match?"

"You think that's a good idea, considerin' what were lookin' for?"

"Good point but how can you see anything?"

"Ain't your eyes adjusted yet? Didn't your momma feed you carrots?"

The trapper lifted the lid off one. "Eureka!" Inside there was dynamite wrapped in heavy plastic. The wicks were waxy with moisture, and the sticks dry as a bone.

Susan Lucknow, who had indeed told her only son to eat his carrots, had yelled into the mine several times, her voice getting louder and louder each successive time. She felt her face turn red as she screamed even louder. She could hear the desperation in her own voice.

There was no sign of Jake here.

A flurry of bats flew out of the dark entrance and scattered into the trees above, knocking a very out-of-breath mother to the ground. She had come a very long way in a very short time and exhaustion was settling into her bones. She whimpered in mild resignation but only for a moment. Steeling herself, she picked herself up off the grass, brushed the dirt off her knees, and pulled the hair away from her face. She retrieved the kayak and headed north, deeper into the Gem Lakes.

The large black bear was more cinnamon brown than anything but he found himself lumped into the "black" bear category nonetheless. He was belly deep in his favourite fishing spot along a rocky river bend that was shallow enough for him to see straight to the bottom. He would stay utterly still until he saw a fish pass by and then would thrust his mighty paw into the moving water so quickly that the fish would never see it coming. The first thing he caught on this day was not a fish at all. He scooped up the brown bottle with his considerable claws and threw it on the sandy shore. He grappled with it for a few moments, deciding what to do with the strange object and then simply bit the cap off with his long teeth. He licked inside the neck of the bottle and was suitably impressed with the tasty treat inside. Bears love beer. This particular bear wanted more so he smashed the stubby bottle with his paw and yelped in pain as a shard of glass pricked him on his sensitive underfoot. He angrily swiped at the remains and his attention was taken by the piece of paper that had the same sweet smell of beer on it. He ate it and spent the better part of the rest of the afternoon licking the wound on his paw.

And then there were five.

Jake was struggling with the extra weight of the dynamite. His shirt was drenched and he hoped the smell that he had noticed a kilometre back was not coming from him, although he had noticed the old man giving him a pained look.

As they trudged slowly through the thick air Jake noticed that the smell was getting considerably worse and he started wondering instead if the old man was rotting from the inside out.

As they pushed through the bush and into the clearing where the suckers had run, the source of the odour presented itself. The suckers were not running anymore. There was blood and guts and scales and bones splayed on every tree trunk. There were puddles of fish mush in every depression in the ground. Not a single red fish was swimming.

The wolves had tracked Jake and the trapper, but had stumbled across the suckers instead. They had ravaged the creek and gorged on the fish. The stench of the guts had obliterated any trail. For now.

Jake shivered while the old man shook his head. "I think we're running out of time."

And just to rub salt in the wound the trapper's eyes caught a glint of amber light through the bloodied creek and plucked out not one but two beer bottles from the freshly chummed water. The caps had loosened and slipped off—no doubt doomed from the day they had set sail. The paper inside was gone.

He handed them to Jake, whose face was etched in disappointment. "On the bright side boy, we're going to need those. They'll be useful yet."

Jake didn't want to hear it. All he was thinking about was how many others had perhaps lost their caps, and were now sitting at the bottom of a lake.

A northern pike, old and battle-scarred, had devoured many a fishing lure in his time. He had not been particularly picky about it either. The pike had bitten on every coloured lure imaginable, spoons, worms, and crayfish. He had also chomped on bottle caps, wooden plugs, and wine corks. It is not hard to see then, why the gargantuan fish did not think twice about ambushing the smallish brown object that was floating on the top of his lake, bobbing there like an unsuspecting duck in the fall.

The big fish had gotten cranky with age and rocketed toward his prey with ferocious power. His powerful jaws and razor sharp teeth clamped around the glass bottle, half swallowing it in the process. He leapt four feet out of the water, and then crashed back down with a resounding splash, all sixty pounds of him. A lone chipmunk that witnessed the whole event turned and high-tailed it back to the safety of a very high tree.

The beer bottle would be the death of the elderly fish but not for another three full days.

Two bottles remained.

Bob was barbecuing smokies for breakfast/lunch when it hit him like a ton of bricks. The kayak. That was the void underneath the cabin that had enabled the dog to shimmy under the cabin. His wife's old kayak was missing. That meant that his wife was missing also, and there was only one place where she would go. The fact that Claire was coming in today was not lost on him either. He had no doubt that his wife had picked this day of all days to make her run to effectively handcuff him to the cabin.

He turned the burners off, twisted the propane closed, and left the half-heated smokies for the birds, or for Buzz, whichever came first.

If there was ever a cloud that would strike fear into a man's heart, Bob was staring at it at this very moment. It billowed high and wide from the horizon to the very tip of the sky. It was perfect white against a harmless grey sky but it was shocking in its enormity. If it had been a black cloud Bob would have been justifiably terrified that another raging storm might sweep through while his wife was gone. As it was, the cloud was causing him a great deal of uneasiness, mainly because it was so unpredictable.

Notwithstanding the cloud, Bob was down to his last fingernail. He had chewed the nine previous right down to the skin. He had paced the cabin floor length to length enough times to wear a path into the hardwood floor. He had a conundrum. Claire was due in at any time but he had no idea when. She was coming in with the Howell family from Lot 8 and he was supposed to pick her up at the dock. He had no way of contacting her to find out if they were running late.

Even more pressing was the fact that his wife had now been gone for a full twelve hours and his nerves were raw with worry. It was getting dark outside again. He was nauseous with nervousness. He grabbed his binoculars, went out to the end of the dock, and looked through towards the landing platform. There was nobody there. He lifted the glasses and scanned the forest above looking for the dust being kicked up by an oncoming car but it was so wet out the rain was keeping the dust down anyway.

He clenched his jaw, dropped the binoculars to his side and turned towards the cabin. He would leave a note for Claire, roll the dice and hope he could find Susan quickly.

He slipped on his good rubber boots and his old, well-worn jeans. He went out to the shed and pulled down his camouflage rain slicker and selected the heaviest paddle he could find. It was not his first time in the Gem Lakes and he had learned from experience that while a lightweight paddle may be easier to carry, you were better off with the heavier lumber if you came across something that needed a good smack.

He took four bottles of bug lotion from the shelf and poured them into his dearly departed dog Lucky's old water bowl and then quickly marinated his socks and his belt in it.

He walked through the bush to his neighbour's back-yard and plucked their aluminum canoe off the ground underneath their deck. He wiped the cobwebs out of the bottom and flicked the biggest daddy-long-legs he had ever seen into the forest. The Mularkys were not down for him to ask permission but he didn't think they would mind. Besides, Graeme Mularky had probably long since forgotten that he even had a canoe. He only used the cabin in the winter—when there were absolutely no bugs around—and would come in by snowmobile. Bob knew for a fact that Graeme had, on more than one occasion, liberated wood from his pile during his winter stays. Not one for confrontations, Bob had left a large cardboard sign painted with the words "I recommend the birch," with tongue planted firmly in cheek, and although it was never mentioned in their subsequent conversations, he'd never noticed so much as a stick missing since.

Last but not least Bob shrugged his red and black plaid jacket over his shoulders and clipped a canister of bear spray to his belt. He did not have time to deal with any de-lays of the four-legged variety. He would spray first and ask questions later if he encountered anything that decided to confront him. He was ready.

He lifted the center of the canoe over his head, and hur-ried past the gas shed, up the rock towards the woodpile, and ducked under the clothesline on his way to the path that led to Timber Wolf Lake.

Jake found a quarter in his back pocket. It had been there for over a year, long forgotten a thousand times over. It had been there since the day he first stepped into the Gem Lakes. He marvelled at the minted metal, a small connection to a past life that couldn't be more useless out where he was now. If he couldn't eat it, make a weapon out of it or use it to fuel his fire, then it was worthless in his book.

After an hour or so of contemplating, Jake figured the coin was good for only one thing. He flipped it into the lake, making a wish on it as it plunked into the water. Even though there was nobody else around, Jake did not say the wish aloud as it probably would have jinxed it right off the bat, but any betting man worth his salt would've placed their hard-earned dollar on something to do with at least one of those beer bottles making it home in one piece.

The clouds were so low they seemed to be scraping the tops of the trees while a fog was lifting from the lake, hanging in the damp air and soon Jake's skin and clothes were damp as well. Through the haze Jake kept his eye on the shoreline as he watched a foggy figure make its way slowly around the lake. He had noticed it twenty minutes ago and it was now getting closer.

His heart was in his throat.

The figure slinked behind the cabin.

The old crow, with a full belly of cold cheese-filled smokies, watched from under a pine bough as Claire stood at the landing dock, knee deep in a pile of her gear and squinted through the drizzle towards her family's cabin.

The cottage itself was shielded by a thin jut of rock and trees, but you could still make out the shadow of the Lucknow dock. She had expected her dad would have met her at the top of the hill, and helped her carry all her stuff down. Instead, she had taken it all down herself, including the heavy cooler full of ice she had brought with her, and the last four days worth of newspapers: two of the most coveted commodities from the city for the information starved and cold drink deprived cottagers.

She had sent the Howells along their way. "Don't worry, my dad is watching for me," were her exact words. If this were a nice day there would no doubt be people out sunning themselves on every dock or beach. There would be people fishing and tubing or playing beach football. Any one of them might have offered her a ride over to her cabin. As it was, gloomy and rainy and pretty darn near closing in on happy hour, people were all inside, lighting a warm fire, playing cards, sipping special coffees or hot chocolate or whatever else. Not one of them was thinking about taking the boat over to see if Claire Lucknow needed a ride over.

Where was her father?

Her dad had never been late in picking her up from the dock. She tried to think of possible excuses like the boat motor not starting or his wristwatch battery dying but he could have always walked around or borrowed the neighbours boat. She remembered he wore a solar powered watch.

Even if something had happened to her dad, her mom would surely have met her instead. It had been months since she'd left on her trip!

She grunted in disgust, resigned to the fact that she would have to take the path around. In the sun, walking around was actually quite pleasant, but in the rain the water collected into puddles very quickly, and the sand and the mud made for slippery navigation. Of course, she had no rubber boots either, as they were tucked away quite neatly and quite uselessly under the bottom bunk of her room.

She dragged her bags back up the ramp of the dock and sheltered them under a pine tree. She left the cooler where it was because she didn't care if that got any wetter. The only thing that she took with her was her backpack of clothes because she didn't stand a chance of being even remotely dry when she completed her twenty-minute walk.

She saw only one person on her trek: Mr. Klosky, from Lot 14, who was in his yellow rainsuit, fiddling with his water pump. From the look on his face he wasn't having much success.

She walked up the path to her cabin a little bit uneasy. Her father would never have forgotten about her coming in today, of that she was sure. Still, she was hoping she would find him asleep on the couch, lulled to rest by the pitter-pattering rain on the shingles of the roof. She opened the door. "Hello?"

The cabin was cool. There was a mound of grey ash in the fireplace with one or two stubborn embers still glowing warm. There was a note on the table.

Although he had not set foot in the Gem Lakes since before Claire was born, it was remarkably clear in Bob's memory. He remembered going back into the woods with his father to visit the trapper who seemed ancient even then. He recalled lying on his stomach in the bottom of the canoe, face pressed against the wet bottom and he head covered while the roar of his dad's shotgun kept the incoming mallards at bay. Playing cribbage on the old antler bone and the absolute ridiculously large fish—the kind of fish where fish stories came from with fillets as thick as steaks.

He remembered the joaquin.

The wolf lair sat high above the tree line, a pile of rubble and rocks on the highest embankment in the Gem Lake range. The red fox that used to inhabit the cave-like structure was unceremoniously evicted several weeks ago—a small pile of bones the only reminder of the former tenant who had proved to be an excellent host, reluctantly serving himself as dinner. The wolves had a panoramic view of everything below them, a heavily wooded forest that stretched for miles and a crystal clear creek that provided them with fresh water. They were hungry. They were always hungry it seemed. An intense cramping ache throbbed in their bellies constantly.

A foreign smell wafted on the incoming winds that nearly made their noses bleed. The pack whined and cried like newborn children, albeit with sharper teeth, and more lethal means. It irritated the leader, nonetheless. He had to find the pack food and he had to do it quickly. He went to the largest of his subordinates and head butted him violently between the eyes as if to say, *Listen up and shut up. We're hunting now.*

By the time Bob had abandoned his lunch his wife was dipping the front of her kayak into the pristine waters of Diamond Lake. She had been making excellent time.

She had hit the shore of Opal Lake, the first of the Gem Lakes, just before the sun had come up and hours before

Bob would even start to consider rolling out of bed. She had figured it out rather quickly and easily found the nest of bulrushes where the old marker was still on the ground by the tree.

Every step that Claire had described in her own debriefing was ingrained in her mind. She had made this trip a thousand times in her imagination. She had a rudimentary map in her head and was now just filling in the details.

She had made excellent progress through the lakes, figuring it must be too early in the season for the freak ducks Claire had talked about, as she saw no sign of them. She took the up-and-over route at the bear caves while being completely and blissfully ignorant of the dens below her, and instead followed a deer path along the shore of Emerald Lake. She had no need to dip the kayak into its distracting and hypnotizing waters. In what may have been the greatest stroke of luck of all, she had been able to easily traverse Sapphire's wind-blown waters in less than twenty-five minutes, and made a short jump to the shore of Diamond Lake without the long leap of faith her children had made off the towering Heights the year previous.

Luck however, is a fickle friend, and the fact that the clear blue sky had shrouded over with rain clouds was a sign that hers was about to run out.

When the first droplet of rain hit Susan smack in the middle of her forehead she began to cry. As the second, third and fourth drop pelted her and the previously sunny sky opened up into a good old fashioned downpour, she fell to her knees, pulling her chin into her chest and heaving great sobs of frustration, which actually took her mind off her terribly blistered heels, brought on by the equally terrible hiking boots that she had never bothered to work in properly.

If she were to be truthful with herself, Susan would admit that her biggest worry was not the rain, or her blisters. It was the *metaphorical* dark cloud that had loomed not to far from her thoughts from the moment she stepped of the back porch hours ago and much like her children before her: Susan was coming face to face with her fear of the dark. It was true that when she'd left the cabin the sun hadn't yet risen, but there was an indisputable difference between "morning dark" and "night dark."

She finally been able to take that first step off the deck and toward her son only by pushing the fact that she would have to sleep out in the open to the very outskirts of her mind. The time was approaching rapidly when her eyes wouldn't let her deny the obvious. The sun was going down. Because of the clouds she couldn't tell if the darkness would come in one hour, or two, or three.

She stopped, relaxed her shoulders, and took a deep breath to shore herself up.

Susan built a lean-to against a rock using broken saplings as a frame and piling on a healthy amount of pine boughs. She arranged them to slough the water off, and then concentrated on making the wall as thick as possible. She was concerned about the lack of a door. Anything could crawl in there with her, and if she was asleep she might not know it until it was too late. She lay on the hard ground and hung on to every moment of semi-light, refusing to close her eyes. Maybe the longer they stayed open, the longer the light would stay with her.

When the sun sank into the other side of the world, it plunged hers into darkness and she listened, horrified, at the chainsaw-like buzz of the mosquitoes rising en masse. They were coming up and out from the forest in droves. She tried taking one of the boughs from the wall to make a door, but it was woefully inadequate. The first of the buzzing bugs found her, and she was forced to cover her eyes and face and as much of her neck as possible from the mad scramble.

They were merciless. They did not care that she was a grieving mother looking for her son. They did not pity her loss, they had complete disregard for her sobs. She cried behind tightly shut eyelids and then the ants joined the party: tiny bites of fire on her legs, under her pants. She squashed them through the fabric, and tucked her pant legs into her socks. Sleep would not be visiting her on this night. She could feel her brain begin to crack already. The mosquitoes made their way through her tangled hair in search of scalp. Any swatting resulted in streaks of blood as the bugs gorged themselves on her flesh, plumping to the size of blueberries.

The spooky figure in the fog making its way around the lake turned out to be the best Jake could have hoped for. It was not a wolf, which he knew was trouble, and it was not the willow witch, which he thought was friendly but he wasn't sure.

The trapper.

He had gone and hunted down four old railroad spikes from the abandoned line, most likely feeling chastised from the moose hunt. As far as weaponry was concerned, a sharpened stick was not going to cut it. They spent an hour or so grinding the steel tips down with granite rocks, and then lashed them with moose sinew tightly to shorter poles than they had used in the moose hunt. They had briefly considered using the sharpened spikes as knives but decided that if they were ever that close enough they would likely be dead before they had a chance to use them.

As they spread their entire arsenal on the grass in front of them, Jake stole a glance at the trapper who looked equally unenthralled. Two beer bottles, two remodelled but tip heavy spears, some old shotgun shells and a couple of sticks of dynamite that might or might not blow up in their hands when lit.

"What's our Plan B?"

The old man snorted. "Run."

According to her father's note Claire was supposed to stay put and not leave the cabin unless it was actually *on* fire and even then only if it were under the threat of imminent collapse. He had specifically mentioned to not even consider following him back into the Gem Lakes. Of course that *had* been her first consideration but the last sentence that he had written convinced her to stay.

Lock the door at night.

They didn't even lock the door when they left in the fall for the winter. Claire had never even seen a key. Her father obviously thought that anything coming to the door after dark wasn't going to bother knocking before it came in.

What could have changed since she left here last summer?

Bob did not stop traveling even as the sun went down and was replaced by the much dimmer moonlight. He pulled a halogen flashlight from his back pocket and slowed his pace, but he forged ahead. He felt safer on the water and his heart rate slowed each time he pushed off a buggy, toad infested shore into the sleek shadowy water.

He was thinking that his wife must have borrowed a tent or something and hoped it was a bright color that his flashlight shine would be able to spot through the black. His main hope was that she had at least stuck to the beaten path and not strayed off and gotten lost.

In fact, Bob had already zigged where his wife had zagged near The Heights at Diamond Lake, and was now looking for a good spot to launch his canoe into Ruby Lake—a lake that Susan had not yet made it to. His spine burned at the base of his neck. His elbows and knees felt their age.

He was careful when he climbed over the walls of the canoe here. As he pushed off the rock he felt a wave of queasiness. There was something about crossing a near bottomless lake that made one feel very heavy.

He was well aware that the wolves he had been hearing all summer were likely on the prowl, but he knew it was a large range. He also knew that the next body of water was Moonstone and that the shiny, mirrored rocks that rimmed that lake attracted wolves from far and wide. What could he do? He had to play the odds.

Susan had been desperately hoping to fall into a deep sleep and not wake up until the light of morning, but here she was, eyes wide open, straining to hear. She'd been roused by something she couldn't identify. On the bright side, the bugs had left her alone.

Unfortunately it seemed she had company of another sort and of much bigger size.

Something was circling her shelter, crunching the ground in heavily padded steps. There was a low pitched droning sound that reminded her of the purring of a cat and the equally low whining of a dog that was about to bark.

That was it—the sound that had woken her.

She snapped to full attention. Her eyes focused sharply and her heart pumped fresh blood to her tired brain.

She tried to see through the spaces in the walls but couldn't make out anything other than moving blotches of black shadows in the moonlight. It could be her mind playing tricks on her she thought to herself. Claire had mentioned the vicious animals that she had seen and she had been very careful to avoid even the squirrels. She caught the faint scent of wildberries and saffron and realized that whatever was hunting her had probably caught the flowery scent of her deodorant on the afternoon's stiff south wind. Although the smell was faint at that point she realized that she might as well have rolled in a vat of gravy and lard. Idiot.

She went to check out the large crack of the front opening only to come face to face with the wolf.

The look in the white wolf's eyes drained the spinal fluid from her neck down and she half-collapsed backwards. His eyes were locked on something behind the shelter and he was drooling uncontrollably. Another animal maybe? A bear? The wolf seemed torn, seemingly deciding whether to tangle with the shelter door or to take off after whatever was behind it. It was then that she noticed other wolves right behind the white one.

Despite the chill in the air Susan could feel the hot sulphuric breath of the animals through the breaks in the shelter. She pulled her knees to her chest and sat completely still.

The wolves outside were trembling, but dared not make a move out of turn until the leader did. He had thrashed each of them brutally after the botched attack on the boy, and the memory was still as fresh in their minds as the bruises on their bodies.

Discipline was becoming his main role within the pack and he was good at it. Very good. He now had a second human within easy reach and it would be short work indeed to tear off the feeble "door" of branches and drag her out into the open.

He had the pack under his full control, however an unexpected visitor distracted him. Unbelievably there was another female on the forest's edge with an energy that flowed off her like a live electrical wire. The pack had spent an entire night hunting in vain very similar creatures around the old mine site and they had driven him mad with anger and frustration. The memory pricked at his irritability and he lolled his tongue in controlled rage. Subconsciously his lips curled back and a blast of furnace hot air escaped his guts and wafted through the lean-to. His eyeshine reflected pure hatred.

All five wolves were now focused on the creature in the trees. She stood tall, turned around and ran back into the dark and in doing so ignited the powerful chase response in the pack. The leader yowled and leapt over the lean-to.

A scream came from within the shelter.

Susan Lucknow thought she was a dead woman when the colorless wolf had let out that medieval cry. It had resonated through her head and clicked a tiny switch in the very back of her brain. She had a life-flashing-before-her-eyes kind of moment and she leaned on her elbows waiting for air to refill her lungs.

Her perspective on her unusual situation shifted and whirred and hummed about in her mind until it all clicked into place. Fragments of misinformation were pulled together into one plain and obvious fact: if Jake was alive, it was by a one shot in a million miracle. She dearly wished he was, but now she fully realized the price that the *proof* was going to cost her. She had left the day of Claire's arrival because she knew that once she laid eyes on her that she'd never risk coming back here. She had bet that Bob would do the same but never considered that he may not have been able to let *her* go, that she may be important enough to him that he may come after *her*. Of course he would.

She had been a selfish fool to step into these lakes and had been lucky not to have been hurt or killed even though that remained a very distinct possibility. Susan did not know what the wolves had chased into the woods, but whatever it was she hoped they hadn't caught up yet.

Susan waited until the black night faded to gray before she left the lean-to. Apparently the bugs were early risers as well. She gathered her pack together, picked some dried-out blueberries from a low bush and looked around, confused.

There were animal paths going off in each direction and she could not remember which she had come from. She pulled at the back of her hair, disoriented, and upset that she hadn't thought to mark the right path. She noticed a small wisp of smoke coming from one of the paths and decided to avoid that one. She hadn't even tried to start a fire. It was not smoke but a sort of smog that seemed to rise out of nothing in particular. It gave her the creeps. She wondered if it was what had lured away her visitors last night.

Susan did not have time to walk down each one and then come back for the kayak so she made an educated guess and tramped down the path she was almost sure was the right one. It was not.

Six hours later, Susan had walked twelve miles and had dipped her kayak in two lakes she had already crossed. When she reached the shores of Emerald Lake she didn't recognize it, and therefore did not realize she was now going backwards. She didn't recognize it because she was nowhere near the marker, and she had no map.

Susan watched the green water swirl into whirlpools; saw the water droplets shimmer off the blade of the paddle like liquid gemstones, and how fluid emeralds dropped magically into the water. She watched them again and again and again.

A horsefly landed on Susan Lucknow's nose—right on the tip—and danced around, before walking up the slope of her nose and onto her forehead. It then followed her hairline to the back of her neck and then found a tender little spot where it ripped away a dime-sized chunk of flesh. The horsefly more than likely saved Susan's life as she snapped back awake and rubbed the wicked bite mark. When she raised her eyes she met those of the buzzard, which was perched at the tip of her kayak. The hideous black bird stank and had what looked to be a maniacal grin on its face. Its beak consisted of two ragged hooks, and its hairless, pimply head looked like a raw, grotesque, rotten chicken drumstick.

She froze in her seat, afraid that any movement might provoke the immense bird. The vulture spread its wings and opened its beak. Its yellow talons scratched holes into the plastic bow. The vulture was nine feet tall, and its sole purpose in life was to eat dead things. Susan got the feeling that this particular bird didn't have patience for waiting, and might take it upon itself to hurry the natural progression along.

The canoe hit the kayak with a terrific jolt that made both Susan and the scavenging bird scream in alarm. She wheeled around to see her husband with a paddle waving menacingly over his head.

The bird saw it too. It gave up on its pursuit of a fresh meal, and grumpily went back to a tree to wait for something to die. With luck it would be one of these two. Or both.

Part Three

THE PACK OF WOLVES SAT on the north shore of
Emerald Lake. They had been waiting more than
a little impatiently for Susan's kayak to drift into
where they stood on shore. They had chased the phantom
woman through the bush all night and had given up only
when the sun came up and she had seemingly burned away
in the mist. Now they had finally tracked their original
quarry down by her florid scent only to find her on something else's dinner platter.

They paced anxiously as the vulture had cut in line, and
watched to see if the big scavenger was at least going to
open her up for them as she drifted to shore. They were in a
frenzy by the time the man showed up in the other boat.

The eagle stomped along the sandy shore, her golden feathers ruffled in a bunch along her giant back. Her large talons
left cavernous holes in the sand and her eyes were glowering
and on the lookout for scraps of dead fish that might have
washed up on the beach. The wolves' all-out assault on the
animal population was affecting the mighty bird's health.

She was tired. She knew where a food source lived, and although she had never even considered eating one before, if it came down to a choice between starvation and survival, well, there was really no choice at all.

She spotted a crayfish skittering along the shallow surf, and had severed it neatly in half with her iron beak before the small crustacean even knew it was dead. There was a mile of beach ahead and she barely even broke stride as she swallowed the meagre meal. Her hunger only grew. The beach would yield nothing more.

Jake was in charge of catching more fish that day so that they would have sufficient energy levels to make the arduous trip to the ridge.

He spent the better part of an hour constructing an intricate minnow trap made of carefully whittled branches, and vigilantly split cattail stalks, until the trapper walked past him, did a double take, and snatched the ball cap off Jake's head and dipped it in the lake. When he pulled it out, there were a dozen feisty baitfish inside of it. "Take a break kid. You're makin' me sweat."

Jake looked down at his cap and then back at his trap and then dropped the trap in the nearby fire-pit to use as kindling.

The old man stretched out in the grass on his back and tilted a ratty old cap over his eyes. He was munching on a blade of grass. Jake rested on his elbows beside him, stretching and shifting until a knot in his back loosened.

The old man seemed tired and they were silent for quite some time until Jake finally broke the peace. "Doesn't this ever seem like a waste of time to you?"

The trapper glanced over, but said nothing.

"I mean, watching the clouds go by for hour on end? Shouldn't we be hunting or gathering or something? Shouldn't we be planning?"

The bushman continued chewing his grass, as if he hadn't heard, occasionally stopping to let loose a stream of green-tinged saliva. For a moment, Jake thought it was going to be the only reply he got out of him. "This is what we work towards, kid. You ever heard of the saying 'a means to and end?' Work is the means," he nodded his head in a semi-circle. "This is an end. When you're on the way to the ridge, these are the moments you need to have in the back of your head. This is what you're fighting for."

As they came to the south side of the shore—opposite to where the wolves had been waiting—Bob and Susan had to step out of their respective watercrafts to drag them through the thick cattails that were blocking the path.

Bob had played the odds like a Vegas bookkeeper and had waited until morning to go into Moonstone Lake. The sunlight's greatest revelation was what it *didn't* cast a light on: Susan's tracks.

On encountering Ruby's clay shore, nowhere was it scarred with footprints, or had the mark of a kayak having been dragged up the sand.

He realized that he had passed his wife in the dark, and doubled back, hopeful in that on his way in he hadn't come across an empty kayak, torn clothing, or worse. When he had spotted the nauseatingly large turkey vulture on his wife's boat, he had vomited. They were scavengers after all. He shook that thought from his mind. When he had seen her swat an insect from her face he had known she was alive and that feeling was like an 800-pound gorilla off his soul.

Bob pulled his canoe through the cattails first, and looked back to see his wife struggling with the kayak. She was trying to push it through, knee deep in water and sinking fast. The bottom was mud, and with each step forward she sank a little bit further. Slimy tentacles of seaweed snaked around her legs. They wrapped around Susan's ankles, and then her knees, and she felt panic bubbling in her chest. She stopped, sinking deeper in the mud as she did so and took in a deep breath and slowly and deliberately bent down and pushed the intrusive weeds down. More weeds brushed her arm and twisted around her wrist, pulling her forward so the tip of her nose touched the water.

She fought the panic that was building in her belly and steadfastly shouted for her husband, "Bob... Bob? Bob!" He looked back and quickly waded out to his stricken wife. He rebalanced her and pulled her up out of the muck almost having to unknot the weeds that held her in place.

It is too bad that Susan had kicked up the amount of mud she had because had the water not been so cloudy she would have seen beer bottle number sixteen which had been secured in the greasy green grasp of the cattail roots just below the surface since yesterday afternoon. Susan, however, did not see the bottle.

The kayak was pulled neatly onto the shore of Emerald, turned there, and left where it was. Bob did not bother tying it up. Susan had wanted to take it back but he was in no mood for negotiation. They would make quicker time back home in the canoe.

Susan, still miffed at her failed mission, was walking several yards ahead of her equally miffed husband, who was disgusted that his wife would take such a foolish risk, especially without telling him. While she was trying to give him the silent treatment, every once a while she threw a verbal spar or two over her shoulder.

Bob, for the most part, was absorbing the beating silently. After the enormous relief of finding Susan had washed through him, Bob had been fighting to stave off the anger that had replaced it.

He was afraid of two things. The first was that they would come across Jake, either dead or alive. If they saw him alive, it might crumble whatever emotional foundation he had been able to build over the winter. It would be too hard on all of them at this point. They weren't ready.

The second thing was the possibility that both he and Susan might meet up with something that they wouldn't be able to handle and maybe leave Claire, who was probably waiting very impatiently back at the cabin by now, an orphan. For that he was furious at his wife although he was biting his tongue on the issue right now.

When Susan looked back, not to far from being able to see the water of Timber Wolf and the boundary of the Gem Lakes, her husband had stopped dead in his tracks. A beaver as big as a small bear had waddled out of the forest and onto the thin path between them. It had very long greasy hair with patches and scratches all over its smelly hide. It had a very large tree in its frothing mouth with two hideously orange teeth as sharp as ice picks. "Ugh," she shuddered. It was a gruesome rendition of the great Canadian rodent, the animal that had influenced the country's history more than any other. Susan tried to shoo it away, but it just hissed, yellow pus leaking out of its eyes. "What is *wrong* with that thing?"

The beaver looked like it was greased in motor oil. It was the most unpleasant looking beast that Bob had ever seen.

He put down the canoe and considered making a wide circle and meeting his wife on the other side, but he didn't want to leave the beast alone with only his wife in its sightline. He unhooked the bear spray from his belt but could not bring himself to shoot first. The beaver had no such reservations about Bob.

The hissing beaver wouldn't let Bob get past. His leathery tail was scaly and coarse and he had dropped the stick and was defending the lumber wholeheartedly. Bob tried to give the agitated animal space because he knew that beavers, even the normal sized ones, were just as crazy as moose were. Despite the beaver crowding him, Bob gave the animal a juke to the left, and then tried to spin around the right—an old football move from his high school days. There were two issues with that however. One: high school had been a *very* long time ago. Two: the old beaver, as rotten and slow as it looked, cracked its neck sideways like a lightning bolt. It sunk both teeth in the back of Bob's leg, just beneath the knee and then thrashed him side to side as the canister of bear spray flung uselessly into the wood.

Susan screamed, and the beaver, seemingly frightened by the high-pitched noise, released Bob's leg and made its way back to the gnarled wood. It grabbed the wood and finished its delayed crossing of the portage.

Susan ran to Bob, whose head had rattled off a tree on the fall down and was bleeding badly. "Oh my God ... Bob, are you all right?"

Bob was white as a linen sheet and staring at the holes in his calf. "I think I'm in trouble."

Despite his threats to the contrary, Bob stayed conscious on the canoe trip across Timber Wolf. A river of blood flowed in the seam of the bottom of the canoe.

Near delirious with fear and anxiety, Claire was sitting on the back porch waiting quite impatiently for somebody to get home. She wanted an update on her brother, but when she looked up and saw her mother practically carrying her father back to the cabin, his leg wrapped in a blood soaked shirt, she changed her mind. If this is what the messengers looked like, the news couldn't be good.

"Claire, boil a pot of water, right now."

She scrambled up, her mother's voice spurring her into action. Her tone scared her.

Susan pushed open the door and dragged her husband inside. He was trying to help her but didn't seem to have much steam left in the engine.

Bob lifted his head off the floor sweating and pale but he smiled. "Hi, baby girl."

"Hi, Dad," her lip trembled, "what happened?"

He looked down. "It's just a nick."

Claire looked as her mother unwrapped the t-shirt. The nicks looked more like holes. They had not even begun to clot.

"We need to stitch it up." Susan frowned, "Claire, is that water boiled yet?"

Bob looked at his wife. "You don't sew, do you have thread?"

"Claire, get the rum from the cabinet."

She came back with a bottle. "Are you going to pour it on there?"

"No, down his throat." She took a quick, harsh swig herself to steel her nerves.

"I need a needle. Bob," she shook him to keep him awake, "Bob, I need a needle, do we have one."

"In the shed, use it to repair the tarp."

"Perfect."

"Might as well use a spoon."

She went to the shed and came back with the well-used needle and a spool of Jake's old fishing line. She dropped the needle in the water for one minute and then came back to where Claire was holding her fathers hand, pressing the shirt into the wounds.

"Do you know what you're doing at least?"

"We don't have time to drive out. We don't have time to flag a train. There are no doctors down. Don't ask questions and look away."

"Oh God...." Bob, not a heavy drinker by any stretch of the imagination, tipped the rum back.

Tears welled in his eyes as the liquor burned its way down his throat but it was not quite enough to completely blur our the fact that there was 6 lb test fishing line being pulled through his skin by the bluntest needle in the business.

When Susan was finished she looked down at her patch-work stitches and put her hand on her daughter's shoulder. "Claire, hon ... run down to Clumps and get Lionel to call for help. Hurry."

The crow soared in wide circles above the water, so high that nobody below even noticed him. He was watching the very last beer bottle, the great brown hope, the last prayer, the Hail Mary, making very excellent progress since Jake had deployed it along with the sixteen others. The crow was beginning to think that this was the bottle of destiny, the messenger that was a cut above the rest. It had sailed past the flotsam and fallen trees with barely a difficulty. It had taken the current past a beaver dam that was under construction and had been lucky enough to take the left fork on the particular stream where the right fork would have smashed it on rapids that fell into rocks. It had been ignored by two eagles and a turkey buzzard, and had come by the same lake that the big pike had swallowed its last meal mere hours afterwards. It seemed like this bottle was earmarked for glory.

Unfortunately, with higher expectations comes bigger disappointment.

Beer bottle number seventeen was spit into a nature-made drainage ditch from Emerald Lake and from there followed the free-flowing current all the way to Opal. It then slipped into the creek that drained Opal into Timber Wolf and all it would have to do was drift on the surface of the lake and maybe wash up on a shoreline and it would have a better than average chance of being found by somebody. Not necessarily a Lucknow. Anyone who found it would almost certainly be from Lampshine Lake, and would surely hand it over to their hard-luck friends almost immediately.

It wouldn't even have to be today or tomorrow or the next day but even years in the future. All the crow wanted was the *chance* for it to be found.

What was unfolding below him could almost entirely be blamed on the weather, a sweltering thirty-three degrees in the shade. Because if it were raining, or even cloudy, it would be highly unlikely that the Merriweather girls—three sisters and six cousins—would not have picked this day of all days to go skinny-dipping in the Bay of Fangs.

The second fang of Timber Wolf Lake was occupied by a gaggle of girls from Lampshine. Some were sitting by a fire, roasting hot dogs and adding substantially to the heat of the day. Most, however, were cooling off in the lake, teasing each other, splashing and dunking and making fun of boys in general. They were oblivious of the two boys from Lot 6 that had been braving the bugs and the heat over on the third fang, and who would be looking through the pair of binoculars that they had brought but for the fact that they couldn't stop quarrelling over who was going to use them first. Boys will be boys. They had caught wind of the girls plan at the previous night's bonfire. They had never seen naked girls and they wouldn't on this day either, as their commotion has stirred up a hornet's nest and the yellow-jackets chased the boys halfway back to Lampshine with some very painful souvenirs.

Rob Keough

Mary-Beth Meriweather bumped her head on the floating beer bottle right after her cousin Emily had dunked her
for the third time. She scooped it up out of the water and
held the bottle up to the sun. There was no liquid in it, but
there appeared to be a note.

"Hey look! A message in a bottle!" Most of the girls ignored her, but a few started shouting.

"It's a love letter!"

"It's a love letter for Mary-Beth!"

"Whose it from?"

"The Mad Trapper I bet!"

"Mary-Beth and the Mad Trapper sitting in a tree...."

"Shut up!"

Mary-Beth tried to twist the cap off but couldn't and
since she was skinny dipping, she had to be somewhat
conscious of what position she needed to take. She yelled to
shore, where her older sister was wrapped in a beach towel,
devouring the last bite of a hot dog. "Anna! Catch this will
you? I can't open it!"

Thirteen-year-old Anna cupped her hands and waited
for the throw. She was not likely to drop it, as she was the
star catcher on her softball team. Mary-Beth was the star
pitcher, and could throw a softball through a car wash without it getting wet—or so her dad said to the other fathers
on the team. Unfortunately, throwing an odd-shaped bottle from the water is much like throwing a shoe at a bear
from a tree. It is not quite a natural thing to do. Mary-Beth
threw the bottle with pinpoint accuracy, but the strength
she threw it with was more than a tad excessive. It sailed
over Anna's outstretched hands, a golden-brown rainbow

of a throw, and landed smack in the middle of the fire. It broke neatly into three pieces.

"My hot dog!" another sister wailed.

The paper inside caught fire instantly and there was no opportunity to save either the paper or the hot dog.

"Nice throw, Mary-Beth!"

"Nice catch!"

"My hot dog!"

Moments later, Mary-Beth got dunked again, this time by her cousin Alexa. By the time she rose to the surface, she had forgotten about the old bottle and its mysterious contents.

Lionel Clump had the only satellite phone at Lampshine Lake, which meant that you didn't have to boat out to the middle of the lake just to get a weak cellular signal if the wind was blowing right. By the time he made the call for help, and followed Claire back to the Lucknow cabin, Susan was pushing her husband down the sand path in a wheelbarrow.

"My Lord, Susan, let me give you a hand. Oh geez, Bob, what the heck did you do?"

Bob was ghostly pale but still deeply embarrassed about being attacked by an ungainly beaver. It just wasn't as glamorous as fighting off a mountain lion or a bear or even a badger for that matter. "Wolverine ... big one ... mean old son of a—"

"Geez!"

Help arrived within the half hour in the painfully ironic form of a DeHavilland Beaver float plane. It was the same yellow and red Beaver that occasionally flew in propane tanks and other supplies into the lake, and a later version of the ghostly relic Jake had discovered in the deep forest. Once, it had even brought in a small piano for one of the more musically talented families on the lake.

The Beaver surveyed the lake, made one pass as it dipped a wing in acknowledgment, and then brought the plane down on the water, needing the full length of the tiny lake to do so. He got as close as he could, cut the engine and paddled the short distance to the dock.

The young pilot opened the cargo doors. "Wow! What got at you, mister?"

"A big ole Wolverine! Tore right into him!" Lionel Clump exclaimed as he pushed Bob down the dock. The two men gingerly loaded Bob into the cargo hold.

Susan wiped sweat from her husband's clammy forehead and whispered something Claire could not hear into his ear. Claire could not make words come out of her throat so she just waved quickly and covered her wet eyes.

"I'll meet you in Kenora," Susan said reassuringly.

Bob nodded and then rolled on his side to shield the pain on his face from his girls.

The pilot pushed off and turned over the engine. The propeller sputtered, choked and died.

"This cannot be happening . . . ." Susan stepped forward. "You'd better go get Mitch."

Lionel looked at her. "Can he fix planes?"

"An engine is an engine, isn't it?"

"Who's Mitch?" asked the pilot, who had pushed his door open again and climbed down to paddle back the short distance to the dock.

Mitch Northcutt had been a high school power-mechanics teacher for over twenty-five years. He also had the distinction of being the only person at Lampshine Lake with any mechanical background whatsoever. So when any outboard motor, or lawnmower, or weed-whacker broke down, it was Mitch who got a visit, dysfunctional motors in tow.

It was a well-known oddity that Lampshine Lake was blessed with four doctors as cottage owners, and cursed with only one mechanic. Thankfully, for the bargain basement cost of a free beer or two, Mitch was always more than happy to take a look.

When it became obvious that the pilot wasn't going to be able to solve the problem, and had called for another aircraft—five hours away—Lionel hustled over to the Northcutt cabin, and found the man of the hour on the dock already fixing the Maxwells' water pump, which had seized after not tasting a drop of oil in more than two years.

"Hey Mitchell, have you ever worked on a plane before?" He took the wood steps down to the dock three at a time.

He shrugged his shoulders, "An engine is an engine. Can't get that bird back up?" He had watched the plane land twenty minutes ago and had heard it sputter on the restart. He did not ask Lionel if there were any news on the kid as he was not sure what the response would be. The plane could have been there delivering supplies but it could also be there to take back something grimmer. "We'll take my boat. It'll be faster."

They crossed the small lake quickly, and as they took the last spot on the crowded dock Mitchell was shocked to see a bloody wheelbarrow tilted on its side. Bob Lucknow was lying on the cargo floor of the plane.

Susan hustled to meet him as he walked down the dock and straight for the plane.

"What have we got here?"

The pilot was young and looked hesitant.

"I don't know ... I should probably wait for my boss to get here."

Mitch shrugged and looked back towards Lionel, who turned towards Susan.

Claire piped up from behind them both and looked at the mechanic.

"Can you fix this plane?"

"I can try ... best I can offer."

Claire looked past Mitch and straight into the eyeballs of the pilot. "This man is going to fix your plane and get my dad out of here."

Mitch was a bear of a man but moved easily along the floats of the plane. The lines in his well-worn hands were etched with oil. He pulled his yellow Flin Flon Bombers hat up; the bill of the cap was completely smudged with grease where he had lifted it countless times before. Mitchell used to work at a fishing lodge in the summers when he was a student and had always helped out the local bush pilots with their planes so this was not foreign territory for him.

"What's the diagnosis?" Lionel asked the grizzled mechanic. He was rapping his fingers against the aluminum of the Beaver's fuselage. Each minute that passed quickened the pace of the incessant tapping. Although it seemed impossible, Bob was getting whiter. He was sure getting quieter.

"Dead battery," Mitch responded grimly.

"Dead battery," Lionel repeated.

"I've been suspicious of the alternator lately...," the pilot offered.

"Well what do we do?" Susan asked. The four were huddled around the engine while Claire watched nervously from the lawn.

"We jump it," Mitch said. "You got any cables?"

They did not. Not even in the car. Lionel only carried them in the winter and Susan knew that Bob didn't even know how to use them. Mitch did not have any either as his wife had taken the car home for the week. There were three others at the lake, none of which had jumpers.

"Well we need *some* kind of wire!" Mitch said.

Wire suitable for conducting electricity was hard to come by at a lake that didn't have electricity.

Susan, who was standing back from the crowd, back at the cargo hold again, red-eyed and worried, spoke up, "Would solar work?"

The three men turned to the smallish woman like she held the answers to every question in the universe.

"Reilly's place...."

Peter Reilly was the first person on the lake to experiment with solar power. Over the years he had added to his panels and he now had enough power to keep reading lights and the fridge going all summer. The system was run by the light of the sun, which was connected to two massive batteries that ran a converter that turned the light energy into usable power. Bottom line: the Reilly cabin was hooked up more or less like a house in the city, complete with electrical panels and wiring.

If they had needed to, the group would have broken in and even removed some wall paneling to get to some wiring. Thankfully it didn't come to that, as a quick check in the unlocked shed harvested enough wire to hook up the entire lake.

"What kind of wire?"

"Anything copper."

"Copper, got it."

They reconvened at the dock and Mitch cut the wire into six long strands and directed Susan to start braiding together three of them. Mitch did the same with the other three.

"Voila. Jumper cables."

"Now what are we going to use to jump?" Lionel questioned. Mitch looked around and nodded past Old Reliable and into his own boat. His eyes settled on the four stroke motor battery. "Twelve volts ... that should do the trick."

Lionel unhooked the boat battery and Mitch motioned for the pilot to get in the cockpit. "Positive to positive, negative to negative...." He attached the bare braided wire to the terminals, and hoped the plane's charging system was in working order.

The pilot tried again. The engine, sputtered, choked and then sprang to life.

Lionel slapped the mechanic on the back and the plane floated away from the dock. The pilot maneuvered to the other end of the lake and pinned the throttle to full. In small lakes like this, with extra weight in the cargo hold, clearing the tree line was sometimes tricky. There was no trick this time. In moments the plane had roared out of the water and back towards the lodge, where an ambulance had been waiting for twenty-five minutes.

"I think that's everything but some shut-eye," the old man announced. He saw a wave of concern wash over Jake's face. He was obviously scared.

Jake put down the makeshift backpack he had been packing and opened the door to the woodstove and threw another log on, his automatic reflex action when he needed to reassure himself. Tomorrow was the day they would leave for their confrontation with the wolves.

The trapper pulled a chair away from the table and stepped on the seat. His fingers barely reached the open rafters but he managed to shift some loose planks around and pulled down a bulky, dust covered blanket.

He took it down and laid it on the floor and carefully unwrapped whatever was inside. Jake was hoping it was some kind of cannon or other heavy artillery for their battle the next day and could not have been more surprised when he the object was actually revealed. It was a guitar.

A mouse peeked its head out of the sound hole and then scrambled out, hitting all the strings with a twang as he made his escape. The old man strummed the out of tune metal strings and Jake immediately realized how much he missed music. The trapper seemed engrossed with the instrument as well, like he hadn't seen it in a very long time. It was an odd sight, the rumpled figure in the corner expertly finger picking a song. And then the trapper started singing in a gravelly whisper and then he hummed which sounded more like a cross between an idling tractor and a broken harmonica. Yet, it was the most soothing thing that Jake had ever heard.

"I'm on a railway to heaven with a pack on my back,
Got no use for cryin' or drink,
Got a friend that I'm meetin' for the first time tonight,
I'll know her by that dress made in pink
Got noone to miss me but the fire I left
And the stars that I watched every night
The clicky-clack of this train on the track,
Where were headed, we'll all be all right."

Jake leaned closer, trying to hear all the words. The light of the fire splashed onto the old man's skin, his character sculpted deep into every line on his face. He had never heard any of the songs that the trapper played that night but ended up humming them for most of the night until he fell fast asleep in his sleeping bag.

Jake woke up early, while the blackness of the night was still thick, and lay in bed long enough to watch the very first reaches of the dawn invade the prized darkness of the room. With sunlight came a new day, and the odds were better than even that this one might be his last.

Falling back asleep proved to be impossible, so he swung his legs off the bed and stretched his arms over his head. He had no appetite, as his stomach was churning badly. He would force himself to eat. His body would need the nourishment.

The trapper had no such reservations about eating, and was already taking generous swigs of tree-root tea to wash down generous hunks of bear meat. His carefully sharpened knife lay beside him. He cracked his knuckles, then tossed Jake a piece of meat, the fat still sizzling from the fire. Jake juggled it around until it cooled. He was not a huge fan of the gristly meat.

"Eat up. You'll be needing that fat to burn. It's going to be a long day."

The weather was already sticky.

They carefully funnelled gunpowder from the shells into the two beer bottles they had retrieved from the creek. Two strips of cloth that had been soaking in lamp kerosene all night were laid out on a log away from the fire. The ragged backpack from the plane wreck was already loaded with the ten sticks of dynamite that they had salvaged from the twenty in the mine.

The ridge they were headed for was above a bog ten miles northwest from Lake of the Clouds. Standing between Lake of the Clouds and the ridge was a gauntlet of terrain so formidable that it made the Gem Lakes route look like an orientation tour of an old folk's home.

It would take the better part of the day to reach it. Jake realized that the feeling in the pit of his gut was not unlike the anticipation he used to feel before the start of a Little League playoff game. Of course, the stakes here were infinitely higher than winning a cheap plastic trophy.

Jake went back into the cabin and returned with Rusty Lucknow's shotgun.

"What're you doing with that?"

Jake felt safe with the gun in his hands even though he had never fired one.

"I'm taking it."

"No you're not."

"Why not?"

"The gun don't fire good anymore. Besides we need the shells for something else."

"Something else? Give me one reason not to take a loaded gun?"

The trapper looked irritated. "Boy, you're givin' me a pane where I don't got a window. I'll give you two reasons. That gun is single chamber—only holds one shot. By the time you shot one wolf the others would be using your arms as toothpicks. Second, them shells are birdshot. You'd have to press that barrel to their ear to kill 'em. I don't plan on getting that close."

"The birdshot spreads. Doesn't that give us better odds to hit more than one?"

"We're in between a bison and a buffalo on that one. Birdshot don't cut it—don't have enough shells to take them all down. Don't have enough boom for our bang. We got to spike our bombs with the gunpowder." He picked the knife up out of the sand and cut open the rest of the paper cartridges with surgical precision, putting the tiny shot in one pile and the powder in the bottles.

He split the pellets between the two bottles and filled both halfway with kerosene. Then he twisted the two saturated cloths into tight rolls and pushed them into the openings. "Well, these should work out just fine. As long as they make it there in one piece."

"They already survived a plane crash," Jake pointed out.

"True."

Jake turned to go get his winter coat, which was going to cushion the volatile bottles during the trek.

"Hold on. There's one more thing."

Jake cringed at the trapper's voice. In his experience, one more thing was never good. The old man held out a ragged cloth, and after he rubbed it on his bare arms and neck he handed it to Jake. "Work this in your clothes. Put some in your hair."

Jake wondered if the cloth contained some magical force shield or shaman's potion that would protect them. He took a whiff and almost gagged.

"What is this?" he gasped. Kerosene would have smelt better.

"Wolf urine. They have a very keen sense of smell. They could smell a ham sandwich from ten miles away. Right now, you're a ham sandwich. If we smell like them it'll mask our scent. We can't stay downwind the whole way."

"Where'd you get this?"

"The day they stalked the cabin. They marked every corner."

They had reached the first break in the forest well before noon. The tornado had evidently touched down several more times after it had buzzed by the cabin and they had been able to walk along the scarred path for quite a ways. Nonetheless, they were ready for a short break. The old man was tired. Jake was tired of smelling of wolf urine, and was tempted to wash it off in the running water that cut in front of their path.

He forgot about the stink as soon as he saw the falls. They were mesmerizing. Vibrant rainbows shone through the mist putting to shame any other a rainstorm had ever created. Some of the rocks were just under the surface and slick with slime. "Wonderfalls," the old man noted. "Not too shabby, eh?" The rocks were right at the lip. They could use them as a bridge, if they attempted the crossing here.

If he leaned over he could see the boiling foam in the whirlpools below. The jagged rocks would slice any man, woman or child into shreds quicker than you could realize that your head was no longer attached to your neck. "There wouldn't be enough left of you to feed the fish," the old man offered.

It was true. If he fell, before he could even hit that violent water his skull would have rattled off several rocks: bone-crushing rocks that would grind him into sediment.

They moved down the shore until they were past the eddies and whirlpools of the bottom of the falls and launched the canoe in a calm pool blanketed with yellow and white lilies. They needed to paddle a ways to hit the next portage. All went smoothly for roughly ten minutes.

And then they hit the rapids.

A huge rock split the creek, funnelling two channels of churning water on either side. One paddle snapped, and then the other cracked. The rock sliced open a gash on the side of the canoe. Jake watched as one spear and then the second bounced from the gunwales, and floated on the surface for the briefest of moments before the carefully sharpened railroad spikes dragged them to the bottom. The trapper cursed.

Jake followed the lead of the old man, who had a grip on the edge of the canoe, shifting his body weight now the only hope of control they had in the frothy water. The backpack was wedged tightly underneath his seat. He prayed that he didn't flip and soak the dynamite. He prayed even harder that the bottle bombs didn't ignite underneath him.

Jake was up the creek without a paddle. Literally.

So they had lost their primary weapons and one paddle. It could have been a lot worse. At least they didn't lose the bombs.

The bog was in the middle of a dense forest of black spruce, and started at the end of a flooded plain of pines called The Shallows. Some very industrious beavers had been at work and had obviously been left unattended. The grey trees were bent over and bare. The effect was full-on creepsville.

The spruce trees were thick with mosquitoes, and the lake was so shallow, and so rocky, and so littered with trees that careful navigation was required to avoid shattering the already beat-up canoe. That would make for a lousy start to their quest to kill the wolves.

"Rumour has it the fish bite people in here," the trapper grunted.

Jake stared at the water like it was acid. "Is it true?"

"Never had the gumption to test the truth."

The canoe pitched dramatically from side to side. Water splashed over the rims. Jake was terrified. If they spilled, one or both would surely crack their skulls open.

But the trapper was a skilled paddler, even with a damaged tool, and every time that Jake thought that it might be curtains for them both the old bushman set them straight. They touched the far shore in about ten minutes. The grass beneath their feet was wet. The short portage was a quagmire of deeply rutted and swampy paths. Not rutted from the wheels of a vehicle or cart, but from the heavily-hoofed animals that called the ridge home. Not surprisingly there we no tracks coming back from the ridge.

Jake's guts felt queasy and his lungs ached, as he hadn't stopped gulping deep breaths since he had left the safety of the cabin porch. Still, there was only so much fear to go around. The wolf den was an unknown quantity; he knew it was going to be the last stand for one of them.

The plan was relatively simple. They had all the ingredients. The only tricky part was making sure that all the wolves were in the den at the same time. That was where they would use the pack's instincts against them. The other tricky part, of course, was making sure they didn't blow themselves to smithereens. Neither of them had any real idea of how long they would be able to hold their beer bottle bombs after lighting the wick.

The wolves were not difficult to track. Their paw prints seemed deep enough and enormous enough to be noticeable if you were driving a semi-truck. Jake had seen paws that made the imprints first hand. Unconsciously, he rubbed the side of his face.

His size eight shoes fit easily into the fresh prints. After an hour of walking and looking over his shoulder they made it to the edge of the bog where the tracks disappeared. Jake was nervous because he couldn't help thinking they were walking into some sort of trap. In the wild it was sometimes hard to distinguish between the hunters and the hunted.

To get to the den, they would have to cross the bog. An eerie silence encased the entire area. This deep in the forest even the songbirds were silent. Jake had a bad, bad feeling.

"Beautiful isn't it?" the old man whispered.

"It stinks," Jake responded quietly. The rancid scum that skimmed the surface had a debilitating smell.

"Maybe so ... but it's brilliant."

"Brilliant? How so?"

"Because the wolves use the bog as a member of their pack—like playing in front of the home crowd in your baseball games. They can overcome much bigger animals in the swamp, especially the swamp donkeys."

"Swamp donkeys?"

"Moose. The wolves wait until a moose is in the middle, stuck in muck up to its belly, and then they attack. It saves them from the possibility of getting a hole kicked through them, or their skulls cracked, like they might if they attacked on dry land. It is genius really."

"It's disturbing actually."

"Maybe so."

The bog was a contradiction of nature. There was an enormous beaver dam on the east side that stunk like decomposing trees and river muck, and yet had elegant vines of wild mint flowing gracefully off the side. Tall, bright green blades of grass and perfect cream-colored lily pads dotted the chocolate brown water, which seemed to be giving off a pungent smell of rotting flesh. In fact, it wasn't the vegetation. The forest surrounding the bog was clogged with abandoned carcasses of deer or moose that had wandered into the swamp to chew on the abundant grass, or escape a swarm of bugs by taking a dip into the water, only to be ambushed at their most vulnerable. Whatever the wolves didn't devour was left to decompose in the hot sun.

The white wolf clenched the skull of a cougar in his powerful jaws. The rest of the pack was feasting on the remaining fresh meat. Almost all of their mouths were bleeding as they crunched through splintered bones and swallowed them. The wolves were only a few miles from the ridge when they came upon the wildcat. The familiar form of the cougar reminded them of the joaquin and it incensed the pack. The fight had lasted only minutes.

The leader stood still and sniffed the air. He had caught an unusual scent on the wind and now he tried to pick it up again. The smell of the ravaged cougar was confusing his senses. They had travelled a long way that morning and had eaten nothing all day. The cougar meat only stoked the fire in their bellies. They would go back to the ridge and rest. When night fell, they would enter the forest and make their way south. They knew there was food in the south.

The two wolf hunters made it through the bog relatively unscathed except for the flowers that had sprayed seeds and pollen at their faces and chests. Jack pines were precariously anchored on the steep rock of the other side at impossible angles. Jake could not understand how they found root. The mud was caked on their pants. They climbed the hill, taking turns pulling each other up rock sections, and holding back thick brush so the other could pass through. Their arms were scratched and punctured by branches and thorns.

They were making their way through what seemed the easiest part, hip deep green grass, when the trapper screamed in pain and went down in a heavy heap. Jake's first thought was heart attack.

The trapper had felt a million imagined bullets pierce his leg, which stiffened, went limp, and then buckled all in one motion. He instinctively grabbed for the pain and almost fainted straight away when he touched it. Porcupine quills stuck like darts in his calf. He felt a wave of nausea wash over him as he watched the offended porcupine with its blunt nose and tiny eyes snort and waddle into the safety of the grass, its quills fanned out in prickly protection. The old man had nearly stepped on the frightened rodent, which had been hidden in the grass. It had lashed its 30,000 plus quill-equipped tail viciously with loose quills flying through the air. Each of those quills had several dozen barbs, and if given the chance to remain for any length of time in the flesh of the trapper's leg each barb would swell, and work itself in even further.

The old man grimaced, and quickly and expertly pulled each quill out, one by one, with each leaving its own angry red puncture mark and droplets of blood. He groaned aloud. The stinging pain was quickly being replaced by a rigidity in his muscles.

Jake was immediately by his side, equally grateful that it was not a heart attack, and horrified at the scene below the old man's knee. Even he could see that the leg was going to be as useless as a wet match.

It was late afternoon, and it had taken them all day to get to the bog. If they turned back now they would be caught in the forest in the dark, right in the wolves' own backyard—the extra-large, bloodthirsty and very much alive wolves.

When Jake brought it up anyway, he was quickly shot down. "That's how the hunter becomes the hunted. We can't go back now. We have to push forward."

Push forward they did, although the trapper was pale and sweating profusely as he dragged his numb leg all the way up the hill.

The trees were lined with crows and ravens. Two fat turkey vultures sat gruffly on the opposite side; the social outcasts of the woods. They all sat silent and still, which cut the end off every nerve in Jake's body.

"Are they expecting a show?"

"They're expecting a meal."

"How'd they know?"

"In the woods something is always watching. Pay them no mind. I didn't come here to be dinner."

The bear with a sliver of glass still embedded in his paw could not believe his eyes when he lifted his head from taking a drink of lake water and saw the white belly of the biggest fish it had ever seen floating just off the shoreline. He lumbered into the lake and grabbed the dead pike with his powerful snout. His sharp teeth sank through the soft flesh, which almost fell apart before he got it back to shore. He used his blunt claws to tear out the bones, and buried his snout in the cavity. His nose hit something cold, hard and familiar. Bears, by their very nature, are very clever animals. They learn quickly. When the Clump family from Lot 7 decided to lock their weekend garbage in their shed for the ill-conceived reason of waiting for a "worthwhile trip to the dump," a bear had sniffed it out. He'd pushed his way through the door's plate glass window, finding the fresh garbage more than worth the effort of the break-and-enter. He did it again for the next three weekends until Mr. Clump finally tired of ordering plate glass and started taking the garbage out each Sunday. There were times the bears seemed smarter than the humans.

This bear remembered the fruity smell of beer. Although it was tough to distinguish through the stench of rotting fish, it was still there. He also painfully recalled the glass sliver, which was slowly working itself out but still causing him to move with a considerable limp. He swatted the bad memory away like an annoying fly, and continued with his meal.

The late day heat had turned oppressive and pressed down on Jake and threatened to flatten him against the earth. He studied the treetops intently for even the slightest hint of wind.

Finally, as they reached the top, the trees thinned out. There, about thirty yards away, and sheltered by a nest of tall Jack pines, was the wolf den. The old foxhole had been clawed deeper and wider and was encased by several moss-covered boulders. From the outside it looked like nobody was home. It was well fortified and impossible to tell just how deep it actually was.

They cautiously made their way to the opening, almost tiptoeing towards it. The stopped a few feet away and Jake shrugged off his pack. They unpacked their armoury.

They had thought of spilling a trail of gunpowder-laced kerosene instead of the bottle bombs, but realized they didn't have near enough. Instead, the old man cut one of the dynamite sticks open and dusted the entrance of the den with the old powder. He carefully packed half a dozen more sticks below the lip of the entrance and gently tossed the remaining sticks down the dark hole.

Jake pulled the winter jacket out carefully and pulled the two bottles from the sleeves. The jacket stunk like kerosene, but he pushed it back in the pack anyway.

"Let's get out of sight," the trapper said, and nodded back towards where they'd climbed the hill.

When they had crouched behind an old, fallen tree Jake's confidence in the plan began to disintegrate. The glass of the bottles had become greasy, as some of the kerosene had leached out of the cloth during the trip. He wondered if they could get a good grip. It was unfortunate that they only had two. Their hiding place was a good distance away, and they had to stay upwind. They waited.

The wolves returned well before dusk, silently and from the opposite side of the hill. The ghostly leader sniffed the air and arched his back. He patrolled the area immediately around the lair's entrance.

Jake thought the jig was up for sure. He fought the overpowering urge to turn and run for one reason and one reason only: the old man was about as mobile as a tree right now. He would not abandon him.

They snorted and sniffed around for five solid minutes, no doubt picking up the scent of the gunpowder and the people who put it there. Jake could tell that their own urine-scented clothing was confusing the animals.

The sun was still high in the sky and right in their sight-line. They had to shade their eyes to see the shadowy figures moving around the rock. The white one was nearly invisible in the beams of sunlight filtering through the trees.

The ghost sat on its haunches and let out a bone-numbing howl.

The wolves retreated into the den.

Jake and the trapper looked at each other.

"Are they all in there? Did you get a count?"

"I couldn't quite see. The sun's too high."

"It looked like all of them."

"It's time."

"The showdown," Jake whispered ominously.

"Whatever you want to call it, are you ready?"

"Who? Me?"

"Yeah, you. You're young and strong and didn't get pillaged by a porcupine."

Jake's stomach clenched. He held out the bomb. He remembered back to the bears, and how he'd tried to scare them away from Claire last year by throwing his shoe. Hadn't been remotely close. The wolves were too far away. Jake would have to get the torch lit and then throw while on the run before it exploded in his hand.

"Ready?"

"Light it …."

The trapper struck the wooden match on his chipped teeth. It flashed and flickered to life. He touched it to the saturated cloth, which smouldered and lit. Jake ran, stumbled, quickly recovered, and calculated when to throw the burning bottle. The farther he was, the less accurate he would be, but the closer he got, the bigger the risk.

He launched the bottle at twenty-five feet, and it looked to be on perfect line. It hit the top rim of the den entrance, and shattered into a ball of flames. "Fire in the hole!"

He saw the white wolf leap through the burning ring of the entrance, catch fire and bolt into the forest. He turned around and saw the Mad Trapper of Lampshine Lake limping straight at him with the second bottle already lit. He was struggling mightily with his balance, and was clutching his bleeding leg with his spare hand. Jake plucked the burning bottle from him, spun around and let it go from thirty feet.

His father would have said that the throw had a lot of "mustard" on it. It also had good line and this one found its mark, directly in the hole. It exploded on the entrance floor, ignited the blanket of gunpowder, which in turn set off the dynamite. The boulders blew apart with an ear-shattering crack, and both Jake and the trapper were sprayed with biting bits of rocks and dust, bone and fur. Heat and smoke singed their skin. They both found themselves on their backs.

The air was so hot that it seemed the earth was breathing fire. Jake licked the salty sweat from his lip. The Mad

Trapper did not move. Jake was struggling to see because the blazing sun was in exactly the wrong spot, and billowing black, acrid smoke plumed from the hole in the ground. It was ironic that a person could be blinded by light as well as dark. Jake plunged his hand into the tattered backpack that he took from the bush plane.

He pulled out the aviator glasses, and pushed them quickly onto his face to protect his eyes from the light and the stinging smoke. The ghost appeared from the forest's edge and loped through clouds of smoke. Its bushy tail was charred.

This wolf was no fool. He knew that the old man was not getting up anytime soon, and that his biggest threat was from the boy. He also knew that young meat was much more tender than old, like that of the trapper's — not that he was that picky, but he salivated nonetheless.

Flesh was flapping from the wolf's jaw, and pinkish foam lathered its snout. Its fangs were freakishly long and wide. One of them had split in two. It was the utter ghastliness of the creature that held Jake in a spell and cost him any chance if pulling off a joaquin-like miracle kill. He sorely wished he had thought to bring the steel fire poker and he could see the crooked weapon in his mind, lying uselessly on the floor by the cabin stove.

The wolf lunged, hitting Jake square in the chest just as he was just getting up from the blast. Knocked back, his skin sizzled as it made contact with the blistering surface of the rock. The wolf was on top of him, hot drool splaying onto his face. The trapper was still dazed and down over ten feet away.

And then the wolf froze.

Jake had one arm pinned awkwardly behind his back and the other covering his throat, because that's what he knew the animal would go for. He braced for a quick ending.

The wolf's glowing blue eyes were looking right into Jake's. He looked stunned.

The wolf whimpered.

The mirrored glasses. He's looking at himself: his reflection. The once proud animal did not like what it saw in the reflection of the downed pilot's glasses — not one little bit. The wolf whimpered again, and then snarled.

At about the same moment that Jake was being pinned by a wolf more gigantic than anyone outside the Gem Lakes would care to imagine, Claire set off on Timber Wolf Lake towards the magnificent beach that stretched for a kilometre beneath the tangled canopy of brush. It was clear of lake weed and rocks, which was rare in these parts.

In the days before bass boats, iPods, and wake boarding, families used to picnic here frequently. The most recent generations had never found the time to enjoy it.

Because of its location inside a large bay, it was an excellent place to find driftwood among other things. When the wind blew from the west for long enough, all sorts of debris in the lake ended up in that bay, and collected on the golden sand.

Sometimes Claire felt that the beach held onto particular pieces just for her. Her grandfather used to carve owls and birds from the wood he collected here but Claire found beauty in their natural state as well. She liked the interesting gouges or hollows. The lighter the weight the better.

The beer bottle lay on its side, shimmering ugly amber. Claire had seen it from the lake as she was coming in, and had only half-interested went over to pluck the litter from the sand. It had not been the first beer bottle or tin can she had picked up. This one was an old bottle, with the cap still on. When she saw the tight scroll of paper inside, her heart dropped deep into her stomach. Her knees buckled.

She did not open it for a very long time because right now, in that moment, it was from Jake. If she took the cap off it might be from anybody else; a joke, a message from some loser boy to another, or anything but what she badly wanted it to be.

At first, it seemed that the wolf's reflection might have scared him away, or at the very least spooked him off of a very vulnerable Jake. It would not be that easy. The reflection only appeared to incense the animal.

The golden eagle came from nowhere and took a good portion of the wolf's throat in a hit and run attack. The wolf had barely enough life left in him to turn and face his attacker before the enormous bird struck again. It was a brilliant death.

The eagle, however, was disappointed. The meat tasted like a corpse, and while usually she might not have minded, on this occasion she did. This meat tasted considerably worse than your average corpse. Although the eagle was hungry, very hungry indeed, she left the fresh kill, and soared high above the bloody and smouldering scene below her. She saw the old man crawling over to the young boy, and pulling the headless body of the wolf off him.

Jake had escaped death for the third time in his young life.

Bob Lucknow and his forty-five fresh stitches had just returned from his medical emergency in a somewhat doped-up state when Claire came in the kitchen with the bottle. Tear tracks streaked her face, and she was taking big breaths as she tried to talk. She had finally found the nerve to see who had written the letter. She handed it quietly over to her mother, who had been examining her husband's repaired limb. Susan sat down at the kitchen table and Bob pushed himself up and leaned against the back of her chair.

She carefully unrolled the white bark and read through the faded pencil writing twice. A tear, then another, fell on the letter and Susan was surprised to realize that neither was hers. Bob looked out onto the lake where the afternoon was fading into dusk. He sniffled and wiped his eyes.

Susan read the words again.

To Mom and Dad and Claire,

How do the Bombers look this year guys? Any chance at the Grey Cup?

Things are OK out here... I'm OK. Grandpa's shown me a ton of neat stuff and sometimes the foods actually pretty good. (Mom, I've got a great mushroom sauce recipe for goose!) Claire—I guess you can have the top bunk now and I hid the jar of coins we collected from beneath the hammock under the fourth floorboard from our window—the one that squeaks (the board not the window!). Spend it on something cool!

Dad—you WOULD NOT BELIEVE *the size of the fish out here! I can catch a Master Angler every day if I wanted! I can clean them myself now too. You'd be proud!*
   I am thinking of you all the time.... I miss you all.
Love Jake

They were quite the pair walking home. The old man with the useless leg and Jake with a separated shoulder, both of them with singed hair, red skin and smelling like the grill of a charcoal barbeque. Neither of them could claim to have eyebrows but both were having trouble hiding the grins that came with getting away with something.

Susan tossed a bottle into Timber Wolf Lake. She was alone, except for a silent crow that seemed to be watching her. There had been a lot of crows around lately, she realized. She shrugged it off.

Looking out onto the large lake, towards the Opal portage, she sighed. She did not have a canoe with her, or a kayak. She was not planning on stepping off the shoreline.

She looked down at the bottle she had in her hand. It was one of her husband's with the label ripped off. She had whittled down a cork from a wine bottle and sealed the bottle airtight but not before she had written a letter of her own to her son. Claire had caught her while she was writing it and within an hour, had produced a letter of her own. Both were now rolled into the same tight scroll.

She had thought about using the same bottle that Jake had sent, since it seemed to know the way, but she couldn't bring herself to part with it. She knew that the chances of this bottle making it were slim, that its chances would improve greatly with each Gem Lake she could cross, but she could not bring herself to do that either. She could have been killed last time, and going out to look for her could have killed Bob. She had come to the realization that both Claire and Bob needed her more than ever now. It was time she stopped leaning on them for strength, and start standing on her own.

She kissed the bottle, sighed one more time and tossed it as far as she could. When the bottle splashed down in the lake, the crow cawed loudly. She had no way of knowing if the bottle would ever even get past the lake in front of her but the old brown beer bottle that Jake had tossed had delivered much more than a letter. It had been full of hope and that was the one thing that Susan had needed most of all.

The dragonflies were back.

Jake was sitting on the bottom step of the cabin, letting his bare feet stretch in the cool grass. The mosquitoes were too busy dodging the sparkling dragonflies to care about him. His shoulder still hurt, although it was better since the horrible moment when the trapper had reset it.

The trapper was back in the woodpile, helping split a cord of wood for the upcoming fall. Every few moments came the reassuring thump of an axe finding its mark. The old man would be leaving that night, headed back to Lampshine Lake. Headed back home.

The comforting sound from the woodpile reminded Jake of his grandfather and he suddenly found himself blinking away unexpected tears. The one-handed man with the wild white beard had been an intimidating presence when Jake and Claire had first met him. He had been surly, sour, and reluctant to open up in the beginning. In the end, nobody had taught him more in such a short period of time. It was not math, French or science that he had learned either, but how to appreciate life and nature and how to have respect for both.

He missed him.

Now, as he sat taking in the view his thoughts wandered back to Lampshine Lake.

Jake had a lot of time to think while he had been away from his family and friends. If he ever found out that he could safely leave the lakes, even for a day, he would have a lot of advice his old acquaintances back at Lampshine and even back in the city.

He would invite them to tie up their shoelaces just a little extra tightly and step out of the back door of whatever cabin they were visiting. He would further urge them to walk past the spot where they had parked the car and ramble past to the edge of the dirt road where the gravel spilled into the tall grass. Then he would insist that they take one more step into the first row of trees and look. Just look.

What is beyond holds the past and the present. In the forest, the future is uninvited.

On the very tip of the straightest and strongest and most splendid of the trees in Flagpole Bay, the crow let the wind soothe his old weary feathers. He could not stay out of the

Gem Lake range for as long of periods of time anymore. He *was* over two hundred years old after all. No spring chicken.

Over his many years he had been shot at more than fifty times—sometimes by irritable early morning risers who thought his cawing may have been a little ill-timed, sometimes by little boys with pellet guns who had decided to move up from plinking cans to moving targets. He had been stalked by countless bobcats, eagles, martins and minks.

The black bird lifted off the branch and caught a wind current up and over Timber Wolf Lake towards the northwest corner. He soared over forest so thick with brush and trees that no predator or human would bother trying to penetrate it.

Behind the protective ring of lumber was an out-of-sight lake with hundreds of crows, most old, some young, all watchers who were a swarming movement of black shadows so thick with feathers that you couldn't see the forest for the crows.

A thin arc of yellow sun splashed a blanket of red onto the mirrored stillness of the water and painted the dusk sky above it lavender. The green and brown and grey of the trees across the lake had been transformed into an undistinguishable solid black base but the colours of the sky coated the feathers of the crow. A ghost ship of white cloud passed between the sun and the earth, shooting gleaming beams of disappearing sunlight into a fan across the sky. The old crow came back to this same place every night. The black birds had been watching over this rugged country for hundreds of years and through it all there wasn't a better show on earth, right here, right now.

ACKNOWLEDGEMENTS

*Special thanks and gratitude to Anita Daher
for helping make this a better story.
I have a new appreciation for the tedious
and unglamorous world of editing!*